THE
SACRED
NIGHT

TAHAR BEN JELLOUN

THE
SACRED
NIGHT

Translated by
Alan Sheridan

A Helen and Kurt Wolff Book
Harcourt Brace Jovanovich, Publishers
San Diego   New York   London

HBJ

Printed in the United States of America

Library of Congress Cataloging-in-Publication Data
Ben Jelloun, Tahar, 1944–
[Nuit sacrée. English]
The sacred night / Tahar Ben Jelloun;
translated by Alan Sheridan.
p.   cm.
Translation of: La nuit sacrée.
"A Helen and Kurt Wolff book."
ISBN 0-15-179150-3
I. Title.
PQ3989.2.J4N813   1989
843—dc19   88-30632
                                              CIP

Designed by Beth Tondreau Design/Gabrielle Hamberg

First edition

A B C D E

CONTENTS

v

THE
SACRED
NIGHT

PREAMBLE

The truth is what matters.

I'm an old woman now, with all the serenity I need. But I'm going to speak, for I feel encumbered. What weighs me down is not so much the years as all the things I've left unsaid, all the things I've hidden. I hadn't realized that a memory full of silence could become a sandbag that makes it hard to walk.

It took time to reach you here. Friends of the Good! The public square is still a circle. Like madness. Nothing has changed, neither sky nor men.

I am happy to be here at long last. You are my deliverance, the light of my eyes. Many and beautiful are my wrinkles. The ones on my forehead are the marks and trials of truth, the harmony of time. The ones on my hands are lines of fate. Look how they cross, tracing the paths of fortune, drawing a star that has fallen into lake waters.

The story of my life is written there, every wrinkle a century, a road on a winter's night, a spring of clear water on a misty morning, a meeting in a forest, a broken friendship, a cemetery, a blazing sun. That furrow on the back of my left hand is a scar; death stopped one day and held out a pole to me. Perhaps to save me. But I turned away. It's all easy enough, as long as you don't try to change the river's course. There is no greatness or tragedy in my story. It is simply strange. I have conquered violence so as to earn passion, and to become an enigma. I have long walked the desert; I have paced the night and tamed my pain.

Friends of the Good! What I am going to tell you sounds like truth. I have told lies. I have loved and deceived. I have traveled countries and centuries. I have often been an exile, lonesome among the lonely. Old age came upon me one autumn day, as my face turned back to childhood, to that innocence that had been taken from me. Don't forget, I was a child whose identity was clouded, unsteady, a girl disguised as male by a willful father who felt demeaned and humiliated because he had no son. I became the son he dreamed of. Some of you know the rest; others have heard bits and pieces of it. Those who ventured to tell the story of that child of sand and wind ran into trouble. Some suffered amnesia, others nearly lost their souls. You've heard stories, but they were not really mine. Yes, I heard them, even locked up and isolated as I was. They neither surprised nor troubled me. I knew that when I disappeared, I would leave behind

2

fuel for the most extravagant tales. But my life is not a tale, and I am determined to establish the facts, to yield the secret hidden under a black stone in a house with high walls at the end of an alleyway sealed by seven gates.

INVENTORY

A fter his confession, the storyteller disappeared again. No one tried to make him stay or to talk to him. He rose, gathered up his yellowed, moon-soaked manuscript, and melted into the crowd without looking back.

His listeners were struck dumb. They did not know what to make of him, illustrious and beloved storyteller that he was. He would begin a story, break off suddenly, then come back not to continue it, but to say that he ought not to tell it, for he was possessed by misfortune.

Some were no longer under his spell. They had doubts. They had had enough of those silences made of absence and anticipation. They no longer trusted this man whose words they had once devoured so eagerly. They were convinced that his memory was failing and that he was afraid to admit it. His memory might be gone, but not his imagination. He proved that when he came out of the desert, face blackened by the sun, lips cracked by thirst and heat, hands hardened by carrying stones, voice as hoarse as if a sandstorm had racked his throat. His gaze was fixed upon some high and distant line. He was talking to somebody no one could see, perhaps perched on a throne in the clouds. He spoke to him as if asking him to bear witness. The audience watched his gestures and his eyes, but they could see nothing. Some imagined an old man on a camel waving his hand so as not to hear the storyteller.

He mumbled incomprehensibly. This came as no surprise, for he often peppered his stories with words in some unknown language, doing it so well that people understood what he meant. They even laughed. But this time there was nothing else but those unfinished, mangled sentences, full of pebbles and spit. His tongue trundled along, then got tied up in knots. He blushed. He realized that he was losing not his mind—he didn't care about that—but his audience. One couple got up and left without a word. They were followed by two men grumbling their displeasure. That was a bad sign. No one had ever walked out on Boushaïb. No one ever went away unsatisfied. He looked down from the distant point he had been staring at and sadly watched the people leaving. He did not understand why they were going or why no one was listening anymore. They had stopped believing him, and that was something he could not accept. The undisputed master of the public square, honored guest of kings and princes, the man who had trained an entire generation of troubadours and had lived in Mecca for a year, would not try to bring back people who walked out on him. Boushaïb would never stoop so low, would never compromise his pride and dignity. Let them go if they want, he said to himself, my sorrow is bottomless; it is a sack of stones I will carry to my grave.

I was there, wrapped in my old jellaba. I watched him but said nothing. There was nothing I could say to tell him of my affection, no gesture I could make without revealing his secret, of which I was the embodiment. I knew too much, and my presence in the crowd was no accident. I was coming back from afar. Our eyes met, his shining with an intelligence that breeds fear. He looked terrified, as if possessed by something indefinable. He froze. He saw me as the ghost of a time of ill fortune. He spun around, hands behind his back. I waited calmly, with the patience of a sage. His eyes seemed more and more anxious when they fell upon me. Had he realized who I was, even though he had never seen me before? He had assigned me a face, features, a personality. Those were the days of legend, and I was his rebellious, elusive creature. Madness had already punched holes in his memory. Madness or hoax.

With all I had seen and done, nothing surprised or shocked me anymore. I had arrived in Marrakesh the day before, determined to find the storyteller my story had ruined. I somehow sensed where he would be and who his audience was. I waited for him the way you would for a friend who has stabbed you in the back or an unfaithful lover. I had spent the night in a room overlooking the grain market, a room that reeked of dust and mules' urine. I awoke at first light and washed at the mosque fountain. Nothing had changed. The bus station was still as black as an oven's insides. Still no doors on the café. The waiter, badly shaven, his hair plastered down, his bow tie askew, wore a kind of tuxedo that had been ironed a thousand times and was shiny with grease stains. He pretended to recognize me. Calling customers by their first names was one of his affectations. As though he always knew who they were. He walked over and said, as if we had known each other for years:

"The usual, Mother Fadila, a nice hot coffee with cinnamon and a corn cake?"

He left before I had the chance to tell him that my name was not Fadila, that I hate coffee with cinnamon, and that I like barley bread better than corn cake.

I ate breakfast next to a truckdriver from the Shawia, who was eating a steamed sheep's head and drinking a whole pot of mint and shiba tea. He belched repeatedly, thanking God and Marrakesh for providing him such a good morning meal. He looked at me as if he wanted to share his satisfaction. I smiled, waving a hand to drive away the marijuana smoke he was blowing at me. He watched a girl ride by on a moped and smoothed his moustache as if to say that a nice young girl, preferably a virgin, would be the perfect dessert after such a breakfast.

He picked his teeth for a while, then gave the carcass to a group of beggar children, who took it into a corner to devour what was left. He got into his truck, turned around, and pulled up in front of the café.

"See you next week, Charlie Chaplin!" he called to the waiter.

As I was leaving, I asked the waiter who the man was.

"A vulgar character. Thinks he can get away with anything. He calls me Charlie Chaplin because my suit's too big for me. He always makes a mess of the table, and he spits on the floor. To top it off, he thinks he's great looking, a real charmer, all because he got a German tourist woman to get into his truck one day. They did their filthy stuff and he bragged about it all year long. He's been stopping here for his sheep's head ever since, on the way up and back. You know, Mother Fadila, guys like that would do better to stay in their trucks."

The square was empty. It would fill up slowly, like a stage setting. The first to arrive were the Sahraouis, selling all kinds of powders: spices, henna, wild mint, chalk, sand, and other ground and sifted magic products. Then came the booksellers, with their yellowed manuscripts and burning incense.

Then the people with nothing to sell. They sat cross-legged on the ground, waiting. The storytellers came last. Each one had a ritual of his own.

There was a tall, thin man who began by unraveling his turban; he shook it, and fine sand fell out. He was from the South. He sat down on a small plywood suitcase and started talking, all alone, with no one listening. I watched him from a distance: he talked and gestured as though an audience were hanging on his every word. I came closer, arriving within earshot in the middle of a sentence: ". . . the taste of time lapped up by a pack of dogs. I turned, and what did I see? Tell me, faithful companions; guess, friends of Kindness, whom should I see before me, proud and handsome, magnificent on his silver mare, capable of facing any trial? Time's taste is bland. The bread is stale. The meat is spoiled. The camel butter is rancid—as rancid as our times, O passing friends. We tell of life, and the lonely vulture looms high." I was his only customer. He stopped, walked over to me, and said in a confidential tone:

"I can help if you're looking for someone. In fact, I may well be the person you seek. I have a beautiful story, but it is too early to tell it. I will wait. So, who are you looking for, a son or a husband? If it's a son, he's probably in India, or China. A husband is easier. He must be old, and old men hang around in mosques and cafés. But I can see that's not what you're after—your silence tells me so. Now, what does it tell me? Yes, I know. You hold in your heart a secret, and I musn't bother you. You are of the race of people of honor. No idle chatter for you. Have a good journey, my friend, and let me close my circle."

I left without a backward glance, my attention caught by the expansive, graceful gestures of a young man un-packing a trunk. He took out disparate objects, com-menting on each one, reconstructing a life, a past, a time gone by.

"We have here the bits and pieces of fate. The trunk is a house, which has harbored several lives. This cane can-not bear witness to time, for it is ageless, it comes from a walnut tree that has no more memories. It must have guided the steps of the old and the blind. It is heavy, and lacks mystery. But look at this watch. The Roman nu-merals have faded. The hour hand is stopped at noon or midnight. The minute hand ticks on alone. The dial is yellow. Did it belong to a merchant, a conqueror, a sci-entist? And what about these shoes? They don't match. They're English. They carried their owner in places with-out mud or dust. And this faucet of silver-plated copper.

It must have come from some fine house. The trunk is mute. I alone ask it questions. Look, a photograph. Time has done its work. A family snapshot, marked 'Lazzare 1922.' The father—or perhaps the grandfather—stands in the middle, wearing a frock coat. His hands rest on a silver cane. He is looking at the photographer. His wife is self-effacing. You can't see her very well. She's wearing a long dress. A small boy, wearing a bow tie and an old shirt, sits at his mother's feet. There's a dog alongside them. He looks tired. A young woman stands slightly apart from the others. She is beautiful. She is in love, and is thinking of the man of her heart. He is away, in France or the West Indies. I like to imagine the story of the young woman and her lover. They live in Guéliz. The father is a civil inspector in the colonial administration. He hangs out with the local pasha, the famous Glawi. You can see it in his face. Something is written on the back of the photograph: 'an afternoon of good . . . April 1922.' Now look at these worry-beads; coral, amber, silver. They must have belonged to an imam. Maybe the wife wore them as a necklace . . . Coins . . . a rial with a hole in it . . . a centime . . . a Moroccan franc . . . Paper money that's worthless now . . . Some false teeth . . . A brush . . . A china bowl . . . A stamp album . . . That's enough. Anything you want to get rid of, whatever weighs you down, just put it in the trunk. I'll take anything, especially coins!"

I took a ring out of my pocket and threw it in the trunk. The storyteller examined it and gave it back to me.

"Take back your ring. It's a rare jewel, from Istanbul. And I detect something in it I would rather not know. This ring is precious, weighty, charged with memories and journeys. Why do you want to get rid of it? Was it soaked in some misfortune? No, if you want to give me something, take it from your wallet, otherwise forget it. Why don't you just go?"

I left the circle without answering, drawing worried looks. It happened that from time to time in my life I would run into people who reacted violently to my presence, to my attitude or looks. I always assumed that this meant that we were of the same type, that our feelings were woven of the same thread. I never held it against them. I would always move on in silence, convinced that we would meet again in the same spirit.

As I was pondering the fate of that family of French settlers taken from the trunk in bits and pieces, I saw a woman spinning around to unroll a huge white haïk that she used as a jellaba. There was something erotic about the way she unveiled herself, as if it was a dance. I watched the subtle, barely rhythmic movement of her hips. She raised her arms slowly, almost as if to move her breasts. A circle of curious onlookers soon formed around her. She was young, and very beautiful, with big hazel eyes, smooth brown skin, slim legs, and a hint of mischief in her smile. What was she doing in this square reserved for men and a few old beggarwomen? We were all wondering the same thing as she slipped a cassette of Berber music into a tape deck, did a few dance steps, took out a microphone and announced:

"I come from the South, from the twilight. I came down from the mountain and walked, sleeping in wells. I crossed the nights and the sands. I come from a season outside time. I am the book that is never opened and never read, the book written by the ancestors, glory to

12

their names. The ancestors have sent me to tell you, to warn you. Don't come too close. Let the breeze read the book's first words. You hear nothing. Be still and listen. Once there was a bedouin people, caravaneers and poets, a people coarse and proud who lived on dates and camel's milk. Mired in error, they invented their own gods. For fear of dishonor and shame, some cast off their female offspring, marrying them off when they were still mere children or burying them alive. Eternal damnation awaited these men. Islam condemned them. God said: 'There are stubborn hypocrites among the bedouins around you and among the inhabitants of Medina. You do not know them, but we do. We shall chastise them twice over, and they will suffer a terrible punishment.' If I speak in verses and parables today, it is because I have long heard words that came not from the heart, words written in no book, but spawned in the darkness that kept error alive."

There were slight movements of astonishment and lack of understanding in the crowd. Some whispered, others shrugged. A voice rose up:

"We're here to listen to music and to see you dance. This is not a mosque, you know."

"I'm happy to listen to you, Madame," a good-looking young man broke in. "Pay no attention to what they say; they're cousins of bedouins themselves."

"A story is a story, not a sermon," another young man said. "And since when do women not yet old dare to flaunt themselves like this? Have you no father, brother, or husband to guard you from harm?"

She must have expected comments of that kind, for she was ready with a gentle, ironic answer:

"Are you perhaps the brother I never had, or the husband so overcome with passion that his body trembles between fat, hairy legs? Are you perhaps the man who collects forbidden pictures and takes them out in icy solitude, crumpling them under his loveless body? Or perhaps you are my long-lost father, carried off by fever and shame, by the feeling of damnation that has driven you to exile in the southern sands?"

She leaned forward, laughed, took a corner of her haïk and tied it to her waist; then she asked the young man to hold the other end. She turned slowly, barely moving her feet, until she was entirely wrapped in it.

"Thank you," she said. "May God guide you on the right path! You have beautiful eyes. Get rid of that moustache. Virility lies not in the body, but in the soul. Farewell. I have other books to open."

She looked at me, suddenly motionless, and said:

"Where are you from, you who never speak?"

She left without waiting for an answer.

I would have liked to tell her of my life. She would have made it a book to carry from village to village. I can see her opening the chapters of my story one by one, keeping the final secret to herself.

The sun had made me drowsy. Now a cold, dusty wind awakened me. I wondered if I had dreamed that young woman or had really seen and heard her. I was surrounded by a varied, attentive audience. People thought I was acting, pretending to be asleep, or that I was thinking, trying to call up the fragments of some story. It was hard to get up and leave the square. When I opened my eyes, they all fell silent and leaned forward to listen. I decided to say a few words, so as not to disappoint them completely.

"Friends! Night lingered behind my eyelids, tidying up my mind, which has lately grown so weary. Many journeys, roads and starless skies, swollen rivers and mounds of sand, fruitless encounters, cold houses, damp faces, a long march. I arrived here yesterday, driven by the wind, aware that this was the final gate, the one nobody has opened, the one reserved for sundered souls, the gate with no name, for it leads to silence, into the house in which questions fall like cement between stones. Imagine a house in which each stone is a day, lucky or lethal. And crystals have formed between the stones; every grain of sand is a thought, perhaps even a musical note. The soul that enters that house is stripped bare. It cannot lie or disguise itself, for there truth abides. Any false word, whether spoken deliberately or by mistake, is a tooth that falls. I still have all my teeth, because I stand at the threshold of that house. If I speak to you, I will be careful, for then I will be inside. You will see me as I am, a body wrapped in this jellaba that protects me. You may not see the house. At least not at first. But little by little you will be let in as the secret becomes less dim. I owe you this story, my friends. I have come just when the storyteller who was supposed to tell it fell through one of those trap doors in the stage, a victim of his own blindness. He let himself be caught in the web spun by the sleeping spider. He opened the gates in the walls and then left them. He disappeared in midstream, leaving my own life hanging. I have given my body to the river's many currents, and they swept me away. I resisted. I fought them. Now and then the water cast me onto a bank, then carried me off again at the first spate. I had no time to think or act. In the end I let myself go. My body was purified; it changed. I speak to you now of a distant time. But I remember everything with amazing accuracy. If I talk in pictures it is because we don't know each other yet. But you will see, words fall like drops of acid in my house. I know whereof I speak: my skin bears witness to that. But be patient. Gates will open, perhaps not in order, but stay with me and you will see."

NIGHT
OF
DESTINY

I t was on that sacred night—the twenty-seventh
of the month of Ramadan, the night the Muslim
community's Holy Book came down from above,
the night when fates are sealed—that my dying father
called me to his bedside to set me free. He emancipated
me as slaves were freed in olden days. We were alone,
the door locked. His voice was barely audible. Death
lurked in the room dimly lit by a single candle. It drew
nearer as the night wore on, slowly draining the brightness from his face. It was as if a hand passing across his
forehead was wiping away what remained of his life. He
was calm, and talked to me until the early hours. We
could hear the interminable calls to prayer and to the
reading of the Koran. It was the children's night. They

pretended to be angels or birds of paradise free of fate; as they played in the streets, their voices mingled with the call of the muezzin screaming into the microphone the better to be heard by God. My father smiled faintly as if to say that the muezzin was just a poor man who recited the Koran without understanding a word of it.

I sat on a cushion beside the bed, my head near my father's, listening to him without interrupting.

His breath brushed my cheek. Its fetid smell did not bother me. He spoke slowly:

"You know that on this night no child must die or suffer, for 'this night is worth a thousand months.' The children must greet the angels sent by God: 'The Angels and the Spirit descend during this Night, with their Lord's permission, to settle all manner of things.' It is the Night of Innocence, but children aren't innocent. They can be horrible. If this night is theirs, let it also be ours, yours and mine. Our first and our last. The twenty-seventh night of this month is a good time for confession, perhaps for forgiveness. But since angels will be among us to set things right, I'll be cautious. I would like to work things out before they interfere, since they can be very severe, despite their appearance of immaculate leniency. We have to start by acknowledging error, the wicked illusion that has brought down a curse on the whole family. Give me some water, my throat is dry. How old are you now? I've lost count."

"Almost twenty."

"Twenty years of lies. The worst of it is that I was the one who was lying. It wasn't your fault. I'm sorry, but I want to tell you something I have never dared admit to anybody, not even your poor mother. Especially not her.

Such a vacuous, joyless woman, but so obedient, always eager to follow orders, never rebellious. Who knows, maybe she rebelled in silence and solitude. She was brought up in the pure tradition of the wife who serves her man. I found that quite natural. Perhaps she did rebel after all, taking an unspoken revenge: she got pregnant year after year and gave me one daughter after another. I was saddled with unwanted offspring. I had to put up with them. I stopped praying and I rejected anything she offered me. When I happened to go to the mosque, I would work out complicated plans to get out of this miserable situation instead of saying one of the five prayers. Sometimes I even felt like committing murder. It was exciting to have evil thoughts in a holy place, a place of virtue and peace. I thought of all the possible ways to plan a perfect crime. Yes, I was evil, but weak too. Evil, however, cannot abide weakness, since evil draws its strength from unwavering determination. But I had doubts. During the typhus epidemic I tried to draw it into the house. I didn't give your mother and sisters the vaccine or the medicine that was distributed. But I took everything. I had to stay alive, you see, to bury them and start life over again. But chance and fate kept the disease out of the house: typhus struck our next-door neighbors, skipped over us, and continued on its lethal way. I am ashamed of all this, my girl, but on this hallowed night the truth speaks through us, whether we like it or not. And you have to listen, even if it hurts.

"A kind of curse had settled over our family. My brothers spun all the intrigues they could, barely concealing their hatred for me. I couldn't stand their polite words, their hypocrisy. But I have to admit that in the mosque,

I began to have the same ideas, and in their place I would probably have had the same thoughts, the same desires and jealousies. But it was my wealth they were jealous of, not my daughters. Pour me some tea, it's going to be a long night. Draw the curtains: maybe that screaming idiot won't sound so loud. Religion should be a thing of silence and meditation, not that din that must displease the Angels of Destiny. Can you imagine all the things they have to do in just a few hours? All the cleaning up? Getting everything arranged? Anyway, I guess they know what they're doing. I can feel them here in this room. I'm going to help them clean up. I want to leave this world clean, free of the shame that I have carried for so much of my life.

"I had ambitions in my youth. I wanted to travel, see the world, become a musician, have a son, be his father and his friend, devote myself to him, give him every opportunity to fulfill his vocation. I fed on that crazy hope, which became an obsession. I couldn't tell anyone about it. Your mother had no desires of her own, or if she did, they had faded long ago. In fact, she was always faded. Was she ever happy, even for a single day? I wonder even now. And I was not a man who could make her happy, or make her laugh, since I was pallid myself, hemmed in by a kind of curse. I decided to do something. A son was the only thing that could give me joy and life. And the idea of conceiving that child changed my life, even if it meant challenging divine will. I acted no different toward your mother and her daughters: uncaring and severe. But I was better with myself. I stopped going to the mosque to work out destructive plots. Now I had other plans, thinking of how to get the best for you, dreaming about

20

you. I imagined you tall and handsome. You existed in my mind at first, and then, when you left your mother's womb and came into the world, you remained in my mind. And there you stayed all your life, until very recently. Yes, I imagined you tall and handsome, but you are not tall, and your beauty is an enigma.

"What time is it? No, don't tell me, I've always known what time it was, even in my sleep; it must be a few minutes past three. The angels must be half done already. They always go in pairs, especially when they're transporting a soul. One takes the right shoulder, the other the left, and they carry the soul up to heaven slowly, smoothly, and gracefully. But tonight they're cleaning. They don't have time to worry about an old man breathing his last. I have a few hours left to talk to you, until sunrise, after the first prayer, a short one, just to greet the first glimmers of light.

"What was I talking about? Oh yes, your birth. What joy, what happiness! When the midwife called to tell me that tradition had been properly observed, I saw a boy in her arms and not a girl. I was already in the grip of madness. I never saw female features in you. I must have been completely blind. Does it matter anymore? The wonderful memory of your birth is mine forever. As far as anyone could tell, I remained what I was: a rich merchant made complete by that birth. But, deep down, in my lonely nights, I faced the monster's unspeakable image. I came and went as usual, but the evil within me gnawed at my moral and physical well-being. I felt sin, then guilt, then fear. All this I carried inside me. Too heavy a burden. I no longer prayed, I couldn't bring myself to do it. And you grew up, bathed in light, a little prince, a child spared the miseries of childhood. It was impossible to go back and reveal the truth. No one, my son, my daughter, will know the truth. It's funny how clearly we can think when death is near. It's as if what I'm telling you now comes from somewhere outside me, as though I were reading it off a white wall where angels stand. I can see them.

"I have to tell you how much I hated your mother. I never loved her. I know you must have wondered sometimes whether there was any love between your father and mother. Love! Our literature, especially poetry, sings of love and courage. Well, I felt no love, not even any tenderness. Sometimes I would forget all about her, even her name, her voice. Total oblivion was the only thing that allowed me to tolerate the rest, all the tears. I'll give her one thing, at least she had the decency to cry in silence: tears would run down the cheeks of her absolutely expressionless face. That face was always the same: blank and flat, her head covered with a scarf. Then there was that slow way she walked or ate. Never a laugh or a smile. And your sisters, they were all just like her. I'm getting angry, I can feel the fever rising. I have to stop talking about that family.

"But you! I loved you just as much as I hated the others. But it was a burdensome, impossible love. I conceived you in light, with a joy inside. For one night your mother's body was no longer a tomb, a frigid ravine. It came back to life under the warmth of my hands, it turned into a perfumed garden. It was the first time a cry of joy or pleasure came from her. It was then that I knew that an exceptional child would be born of that embrace. I believe in the power our thoughts can have when we undertake some important deed. On that night I decided I would be more attentive to your mother. The pregnancy was normal. One day I found her lifting a heavy trunk. I rushed to stop her: she was risking the life of the child of light she was bearing for me. After your birth, of course, I paid no particular attention to her. Our relations of silence, sighs, and tears returned to normal. The old silent hate came back. I spent all my time with you. She grew heavy and fat, locked herself in her room, and no longer spoke to anyone. I think that worried your sisters, who were left to their own devices. As for me, I just watched the drama unfold. I acted indifferent, but in fact I wasn't pretending. I really didn't care. I felt like a stranger in that house. You were my joy, my light. I learned to take care of a child. Which is not done around here. Yet I considered you as half an orphan. After the fake 'circumcision' I started to lose my mind. Doubt infected my passion. I, too, kept to myself, sinking into silence. You were a carefree child, running from room to room, making up games, always by yourself. Sometimes you even played with dolls. You dressed up as a girl, as a nurse, as a mother. You liked dressing up. I kept having to remind you that you were a little boy. You laughed at me. You made fun of me. My image of you faded in and out, clouded by your games. It was like the wind lifting a cloth draped over a treasure chest. A strong wind would blow it off completely. You would seem distraught, frightened, but then you would calm down again. How wise was that little body that eluded every caress. Do you remember how anxious I got when you pretended to disappear? You used to hide in that painted wooden trunk to get out of God's sight. When you were taught that God was everywhere, that He knew and saw everything,

23

you did all you could to escape His presence. You were afraid of it, or maybe you were just pretending, I don't know which."

He closed his eyes. His face was resting against mine. He was asleep. I checked his breathing: his chest moved so faintly that the thick white woolen blanket hardly budged. I lay there waiting anxiously for his last breath, the final sigh that would give up the soul. I thought I ought to leave the window ajar to let it out. But he gripped my arm just as I was about to get up. Even in the depths of his sleep he held me. Once more I was a prisoner of one of his plans. An uneasy feeling of fear came over me. I was in the grip of a dying man. The candlelight was fading. Morning was slowly coming down from the sky. The stars must be dimming. I thought about what he had been telling me. What kind of forgiveness could I offer him? Pardon can come from the heart, from the mind, or from mere indifference. My heart had hardened long ago. My mind had already stopped me from leaving the bedside of this man bargaining with death. Indifference can yield nothing or everything, and I had not reached that state of lack of care for myself. I had no choice but to listen to this man's last words and to watch over him as he slept. I was afraid that I would fall asleep myself and wake up holding hands with death. Outside the chanting of the Koran had stopped. The children had gone home. The prayers were over. The Night of Destiny was about to hand the keys of the city back to the day. Light—faint, soft, and subtle—was slowly settling on the hills, terraces, and cemeteries. A canon went off at sunrise, signaling the start of the fast. My father woke up with a start. The fear had left his face, but now there was panic: his time

24

had come. For the first time I witnessed death at work, as it moved back and forth over the outstretched body, missing nothing. Any being tries to resist. My father had a look of supplication: he wanted one more hour, or even just a few minutes. He still had something else to tell me:

"I saw my brother in my sleep. His face was half yellow, half green. He was laughing. I think he was taunting me. His wife was standing behind him egging him on. He was threatening me. I didn't want to tell you about those two monsters tonight, but I have to warn you. They are ruthless and rapacious. They feed on hatred and wickedness. They are fearsome: greedy and heartless, hypocritical and cunning, with no pride at all. They spend their lives piling up money and stashing it away. They will stoop to anything and stop at nothing. My father was ashamed of that son of his. 'Where does he get that viciousness from?' he would ask me. A disgrace to the family. He pretends to be poor and waits until the market is about to close, then buys vegetables for next to nothing. He bargains for everything, complains, cries when he has to. He always says that I'm the cause of his misfortune, that it's my fault he's poor. Once I heard him talking to a neighbor. 'My older brother stole my share of the inheritance,' he said. 'Even when he dies, I won't have the right to inherit from him, because he's just had a son. I will take my case to God, for He alone can give me justice, here or in the afterlife.' Every once in a while they would invite us over for lunch. His wife would hardly cook the meat, smothering it in a pile of vegetables. The meat was so hard it would lay on the plate untouched. The next day she would cook it properly for her own family. She wasn't fooling anyone. Neither one of them has any shame at all. Be careful, stay away from them, they're evil."

He paused, then began to talk more rapidly. I didn't understand it all. He thought it was important, but his gaze wandered, drifting to the other side of the room and back. He was still squeezing my hand.

"All I ask is that you forgive me," he said. "Then let Him who owns my soul take it where He will, to His flowered gardens and placid rivers, or to a volcano's crater. But grant me this favor: forget me, for that is forgiveness. You are free now. Go away, leave this cursed house; travel, and live! Live! And don't come back to see the disaster I am leaving behind. Forget, and take the time to live. Forget this city! Tonight I have come to realize that you will have a better fate than any of the women of this country. I see that clearly now, and I speak the truth. I see your face haloed in a wondrous light. This, the twenty-seventh night of Ramadan, is the night of your birth. You are a woman. Let your beauty guide you. You have nothing to fear now. The Night of Destiny names you Zahra, flower of flowers, grace, child of eternity. You are time standing on the slope of silence, at fire's peak, among the trees, on the face of heaven descending."

He leaned forward and held me. "I can see you, my daughter, I can see your hand held out to me. You are taking me with you, but where? I don't have the strength to follow you. I love the way your hand comes close to my eyes like that. It's dark, dark and cold. Where are you, where is your face? I can't see you anymore. Is that you pulling at me? What is this white field, is it snow? But wait, it's not white anymore. I can't see anything now. Are you frowning, are you angry? You're in a hurry. Does this mean you forgive me, Zah . . . ra?"

A ray of sunlight came into the room. It was all over. Laboriously, I took my hand from his. I pulled the sheet over his face and blew out the candle.

A
BEAUTIFUL
DAY

A fter that exceptional night, my friends, the days took on new colors, the walls picked up new songs, the stones released echoes long held back, and bright light flooded the terraces. The cemeteries fell silent.

Everything got quiet, and seemed changed. It was hard not to notice the coincidence: an old man finally left this life and an almost supernatural brightness flooded people and things.

Apparently the Night of Destiny, however terrible for some, could set others free. The dead and the living meet at that point where the sounds of the latter drown out the former's prayers. On such a night, my friends, who can tell the difference between ghosts and angels, between those arriving and those departing, between the heirs of time and the callow guardians of virtue?

Think of those carts with bodies piled high inside, some of them still breathing but intent on making the trip anyway, for one reason or another. Walls tremble as the carts pass, drawn by sturdy mares toward unknown places. On that night it was said that paradise was promised to whoever tried to make the journey, or at least to those who would give away their fortunes and the few days or weeks they had left to live, making an offering to that night without stars, when the sky opens and the earth moves a little faster. The people who came to lay on the carts had no fortunes but a pinch of time. Everyone else clung to money and to illusion.

I watched the procession from the little window. They had to leave the city before sunrise. The morning of that twenty-seventh day of fasting was like any other. There was to be no trace of the nocturnal cleansing. I looked at my father, his body lighter now, emptied of substance. I told myself that with a little luck his soul would be in one of the last carts. Weary but relieved, I sat on the edge of the bed and wept, but with exhaustion, not sadness. I was free now, but things were not to go as I had hoped.

I was a woman again, or at least recognized as such by my father, but I still had to play the game, acting as a son until all matters of inheritance had been settled. The house was a wreck. New cracks seemed to have opened in the walls overnight. Everything had changed in just a few hours. My sisters were weeping like professional mourners. My mother, dressed in white, was acting the part of the bereaved. My uncles were busy preparing the funeral. And as for me, I simply waited, secluded in the room.

It was a sunny spring day. Spring is carefree in our country. It changes the bougainvilleas, highlights the colors in the fields, makes the sky a little bluer, fills the trees, and turns its back on sorrowful women. Which is what I was. But that year I decided to put everything that was tormenting me out of my mind. I seldom laughed and was never funny. But I did want to be a part of the spring.

It was hard, my friends, that much I admit. To be cheerful meant changing my face, changing my body. I had to learn new gestures, to walk fluidly. That day's unusual heat reinforced my conviction: spring was not in the house, but it was there outside. Scents and odors came to me from neighboring houses and gardens. The desolation in our house had a bitter, stifling smell. The incense my uncles were burning was of poor quality. What was supposed to be paradise wood was actually some mediocre stick flavored with perfume that augured ill. The three people hired to bathe the corpse were in the usual hurry. They skimped on the water and then got into an argument with my uncle, who tried to bargain over their wretched wages. Their haggling with my uncle drowned out the chanting from the Koran and was at once shameful and ridiculous. It finally got so absurd that I could not help laughing.

"You want to clean out our pockets just to wash the corpse?"

"One thing's for sure: no one will wash you the day you die; you'll leave filthy, and even if you get to paradise,

31

you'll stink so bad they won't let you through the gate. That's what happens to misers."

My uncle turned white, muttered a prayer, and paid the three men their asking price. I watched jubilantly from the window. Someone drew my uncle off into a corner: it was his wife, mistress of avarice, hatred, and intrigue. A fearsome woman. I'll tell you about her too someday, for her fate deserves a comment. She was furious with her husband for having paid the washers.

I had to be the invisible son for another day or two. Dressed in white, I presided over the funeral. I wore dark glasses and covered my head with the hood of my jellaba. I didn't say a word. People leaned over to greet me, to express their condolences. Furtively they kissed my shoulder. Everyone was intimidated, which suited me fine. At the great mosque, of course, I was expected to lead the prayer for the dead. I did so with an inner joy and barely concealed pleasure. I was a woman gradually taking her revenge on a society of spineless men. At least that's what the men in my family were. As I bent down low I couldn't help thinking of the animal desire my body, especially in that position, would have aroused in those men if they had only known that they were praying behind a woman. Not to mention the ones who start playing with themselves the moment they see any rear end thus presented, male or female.

The death rite went off without incident. What I remember best about that day was our arrival at the cemetery. A blazing sun had created an eternal springtime. The graves were covered with bright green wild grass, the poppies were enchanted by the light, and geraniums had been scattered by some anonymous hand. The modest yet immutable presence of a few hundred-year-old olive trees were meant to assure that the souls in that garden would remain at peace. A Koranic cantor had dozed off on a grave. Children played in the trees. Two lovers hid behind a gravestone high enough to let them kiss without being seen. A young student was reading *Hamlet*, walking back and forth and waving his arms. A woman in a wedding dress dismounted from a white horse. A horseman in a blue, southern-style gandoura crossed the cemetery on his mare. He seemed to be looking for someone.

The procession scattered as we arrived. Some shielded their eyes with their arms, unable to bear the intense light. The dead man was forgotten. The gravediggers began to look for the grave they had prepared. Children in the street who had followed the procession began to dance. They approached the body as if in a ballet, picked it up, and turned in a circle, humming an African chant. Then, moving slowly, they placed it in one of the graves that had been dug that morning. The gravediggers, appalled, chased the children away with spades and picks. The bride came toward me and draped her magnificent gold-embroidered burnoose around my shoulders. "He is waiting for you on a white mare with gray spots," she whispered. "Go and join him. Don't ask me why, just go. And be happy." She disappeared. What was she? An apparition, an image, a piece of a dream, a voice, a lapse of time escaped from the twenty-seventh night? I was still dazzled when a powerful arm coiled around my waist and lifted me up. The handsome horseman pulled me onto his mare. No one spoke. I was carried off, as in the tales of old. We galloped across the cemetery. I glanced back at my father's corpse, which the gravediggers were now lifting out of the ground in order to bury it according to the rules of Islam. I also saw my uncles, gripped with panic, backing out of the cemetery.

It was a beautiful day.

THE
PERFUMED
GARDEN

O moon of moons, star full of night and light, this gold-embroidered burnoose is your residence, the roof of your house, the wool of which your dreams are woven, the warm blanket for long winter nights when I'm away. But I will never leave you, for I have waited too long to leave you even for a single night."

We rode for an entire day. He spoke to me now and then, saying the same thing again and again, calling me "princess of the South," or "moon of moons" or "first morning light." I sat behind him, wrapped in the burnoose, my arms around his waist. The mare's motion made my crossed arms stroke his firm belly up and down.

I felt strange, and abandoned myself to the feeling, asking no questions. It was like one of those dreams that continues when you're half awake. I had never been on a horse before. Emotion rose within me in an inner freedom that warmed my body. Adventure is first of all that sense of strangeness of which pleasure is born. I rested my head against his back, shut my eyes, and hummed a childhood song. The day before I had helped a dying man's soul ascend to heaven, and now here I was holding tight to an unknown man, perhaps a prince sent by the angels of that twenty-seventh night, a prince or a tyrant, an adventurer or a bandit of stony paths, but a man—a man whose eyes I had barely seen, for he was veiled.

The slave, just free, was being carried off, perhaps to a new prison, a castle with high, thick walls guarded by armed men, a castle without gates or windows, just an entrance with a stone or two that could be moved aside to let the horseman and his prey get in.

I dozed, dreamed, forgot. A cool wind stroked my cheeks wet with tears of joy. The sky was blue, red, mauve, as the sun went down. I was neither hungry nor thirsty on that day of fasting. My horseman stopped for a moment and said, as if I knew all about his daily life:

"We're going to stop and see the children. If we're lucky, we can break the fast with them."

"What children?"

He didn't answer.

The village was in a small valley that we entered through a secret path. Obstacles had been set up and were guarded by children. There was a password for each one, made up of four sentences that formed a poem my horseman knew by heart:

We are the children, the guests of the earth.
Of earth we are made, to earth we will return.
Here on this earth, happiness lasts not,
But nights of joy erase the pain.

I did not realize it at first, but it was a poem by Abu-l'Ala al-Ma'arri. I had read *Risalat al-Ghufran* in my adolescence, but I didn't remember those lines. That evening one of the children asked my horseman:

"Well, Sheikh, how was hell? What did the dead tell you, and what did the damned do to you?"

"I'll tell you all about it after supper."

It was a village of children. We were the only adults. Simple houses made of red clay. There must have been about a hundred children, both boys and girls. The terraced gardens were remarkably well kept. It was a self-sufficient community, far from town and roads, far from the country itself, perfectly organized, with no hierarchy, police, or army, and no written laws. It was a little republic, dreamed and lived by children. I was astonished. My horseman sensed my impatience: I wanted to understand. We found a place to talk alone. He took off his veil and I saw his face for the first time. I looked closely at his features as he spoke: large brown eyes; thick, regular eyebrows; delicate lips; a lush moustache; smooth, dark brown skin. He spoke softly, without really looking at me.

"I have seven secrets," he said. "To earn your friendship and forgiveness for having carried you off, I will tell you about them one by one. This will take time, for we must get to know one another and allow friendship into our hearts. This village is my first secret. No one knows of it. Only those whose hearts have suffered and who

37

have no illusions about the human race live here. We hardly ever explain the secret, but I owe you a minimum of enlightenment to soothe your anxieties."

"But I don't feel anxious."

That was true. Not only was my mind free of fear, but I felt a deep harmony between image and reflection, between body and shadow, between a dream that had filled my lonely nights and this story I was living out in happy curiosity. I was like a child on its first trip.

That first night was the beginning of an astonishing adventure. My horseman, whom everybody called the Sheikh, had to report on his mission. He had been away from the village for a long time.

A wide-eyed boy with red hair, barely ten years old, came up to me and said:

"Welcome! I represent friendship, and possibly love."

"What are you supposed to do?" I asked.

"To really understand how things work in this village, you have to start by forgetting where you come from and how you lived back there, on the other side of the valley. Here we are ruled by principles and feelings. Forgetting is the first principle. Whether you have lived a hundred years or a hundred days, when you enter this place you have to wipe your memory clean. If you can't manage it, we have plants that can help."

"But exactly what do you do here?"

"I grow the plants that foster feelings of plenitude and harmony. What we all have in common here is that we have all suffered from injustice; here we have a chance to make time stand still and repair the damage. This village is actually a ship, a ship that sails stormy seas. We have no link at all to the past, to dry land. The village is an island. Every now and then we send the Sheikh out to gather information. Often he brings back abandoned or runaway children. This is the first time he's brought us a princess. Welcome!"

The redhead kissed my hand and disappeared. A dark-skinned girl with curly hair came over to me. I must have been a real curiosity. She looked at me without a word, walked around me, ran her hand over my burnoose. Then she came closer and whispered as if we were old friends:

"Don't let the Sheikh get to you; he's too handsome and charming. In time you'll find out how to deal with men. It's not a problem here. We're all children, and we stay children. It's simple. And convenient."

She saw the Sheikh coming and ran off, saying as she left:

"I hope you'll stay with us."

I too began to call my horseman "the Sheikh." Yet he was not old, had no white beard, and looked more like an athlete in training.

He brought us dinner: rich soup, dates, and dried figs.

I was so tired that I fell asleep just after eating, wrapped in my burnoose. The night was peopled with dreams one inside the other, like Chinese boxes. Everything was all mixed up. When I woke up the next morning, I couldn't tell the difference between dreams and what I now saw before me. The grass, flowers, trees, birds, streams—everything around me—fired my imagination and troubled my senses. I decided to give up trying to distinguish the real from the imaginary or to find out where I was. From my window I saw the Sheikh carrying wood while the children worked the land, cleaned the village, and prepared food. Everyone had something to do. I went out to look around the village in daylight. Some of the children smiled at me, others stopped and greeted me with clasped hands. I was learning to walk naturally, without tension, not worrying about people looking at me. I was rediscovering a surprising innate elegance. My body was breaking free of itself. Cords and strings were unraveling, and I could feel my muscles loosening. I breathed more easily. I ran my hand over my small breasts. It felt good. I massaged them, trying to make them bigger, to make them jut out proudly and excite passersby. I remembered those days long ago when Lalla Zineb, an enormous woman who lived with some neighbors, would come over to help my mother out. She would take me in her arms, wedge my small head against her heavy breasts, and squeeze me against her, in joy or in desire. She had no children of her own, and her husband had left her for two other wives who gave him many. So she would hold me close, carry me on her back, pat my cheeks, grip me between her parted thighs. I was her toy. She sweated a lot and never realized that I found her disgusting. I never told her. Her games were a change from the comfort and attention that was showered upon me in the family. One day my father came in unexpectedly and saw me wriggling between Lalla Zineb's fat thighs. He ran over, snatched me away, and slapped the poor woman. Yes, she had huge breasts. They spilled out all over. I began to dream about those masses of flesh, Allah's bounty.

I touched my breasts. They were swelling slowly. I opened my blouse to present them to the morning wind, to the caressing breeze. I had gooseflesh and the nipples hardened. The wind blew all over my body. My blouse puffed out. I undid my hair. It was not very long, but the wind was good for it. I walked on without knowing where I was going. A wild desire came over me. I took off my saroual, then my underpants, to please the wind, to please myself, to feel the cool, light touch of the morning breeze on my belly, rousing my senses. I was in a wood. Nature was at peace. These were my first steps as a free woman. Freedom was that simple: to go for a morning walk and to cast off these binding clothes without asking permission. Freedom was giving my body to the wind, the light, the sun, in happy solitude. I took off my slippers. I tread on sharp pebbles, but felt no pain. I came to a clearing and sat down on a mound of damp earth. A coolness rose within me like a wave of pleasure. I rolled in the leaves, feeling slightly dizzy. I ran to a lake. I hadn't known that there was a lake and a spring behind the wood, but nature was infusing me with new instincts, new reflexes. My body needed water. I took off my gandoura and dived into the water. I had never learned to swim, and now I almost drowned. I clung to a branch and made my way to the spring, where I sat and turned my back to the jet of cold, clean water. I was dreaming. I was happy, delirious, all new and alert. I was life, pleasure, desire; I was the wind in the water, the water in the earth, the water purified, the earth ennobled by the spring. I trembled with joy. My heart beat wildly as I gasped for breath. I had never felt so much before. My body, which had been dull and deserted, a ruin, at the mercy of lies, was coming back to life. Before I knew it I was screaming as loud as I could, "I'm alive . . . alive! . . . My soul has come back, and it cries from my chest, I'm alive, alive!"

Naked children dove laughing into the lake. They gathered around me, repeating after me, "She's alive, alive." Other children waited on the bank holding a white bath towel. They wrapped me in it, had me sit on a wicker chair, and carried me to my room, where the Sheikh, dressed all in white, greeted me. I was still trembling with the cold, and with emotion. I was weary, happy, astonished. Things had happened fast, as though time was impatient. The Sheikh kissed my hand. I laid my head on his knee. He stroked my wet hair as he spoke to me:

"I'm glad you found the spring. That was the second secret. Now you can't go back anymore. The water of that spring does good. It works miracles. And you found it on your own. You are on the way. Whatever you do, don't turn around. It might be dangerous to look back. No, you won't be cursed, as in the legend; you won't turn into a pillar of salt or sand. But you could do harm. And to do harm is a mistake; it is to suffer a joyless fate, devoid of truth and desire. Believe me, princess, I know whereof I speak."

Suddenly the Sheikh fell silent. When I looked up, I saw tears running down his cheeks. He was weeping in silence, his eyes closed. I shivered. I got up and draped the gold-embroidered burnoose around his shoulders. He dozed off, but tears continued to run down his cheeks. Sweet tears. Tears that must have been long in coming. I was intrigued by his serenity, his placid submission to this uncontrollable outburst. I had no wish to disturb him by asking questions. On the shelf a large notebook lay open, the writing inside delicate. There were drawings, signs, questions. I was tempted to read it, but I didn't dare. That would have been worse than theft. I had a

42

sudden, violent foreboding: misfortune lurked all around us. The dream had been too beautiful; now the nightmare was on its way. Four or five children rushed into the room and ordered me out of the valley:

"You made the Sheikh shed tears. You may be one of those beings from the past who helped tear away his soul, his breath, his life. You have to go before he wakes, before he gets violent."

I tried to absolve myself, to tell them that I had torn nothing away, that it had happened of its own, that I had no idea why he was crying. In vain. The children looked at me vindictively, their eyes filled with hate and violence. I went to the Sheikh to wake him up. One of the children jumped on me and knocked me down:

"Leave him alone. He may be dying. He can't disappear again and leave us for years!"

Thus was I driven from the so-called perfumed garden. Believe me, my friends, this was no dream, I lived it. I slept with the animals that night, in the stable on the edge of the village. Puzzled and upset, I spent the night trying to understand, but the more I thought, the darker were the shadows that settled over my mind. In the middle of the night, the red-haired boy, the one who had welcomed me so kindly, came into the stable. I wasn't surprised. I was expecting him.

"Don't try to understand," he said. "I'll help you get out of here. The Sheikh is our emblem; our fate is bound to his. If he succumbs to temptation we are lost. There is a pact, an oath, between us: never to reveal our seven secrets to a stranger. Every secret he reveals is a piece out of our skin. We lose color from our faces, and our teeth fall out, then our hair; then we lose our blood, our

43

minds, our souls, and finally our lives. It isn't your fault. You are good. But something about you brings destruction. I don't know what it is, but I can feel it. Misfortune must dwell within you, unbeknownst to you. It feeds on others' failures and that way spreads. As you must have noticed, we are a tribe outside time. That is our strength, and our weakness. The Sheikh alone is still immersed in time. He grows, gets restless, and ages. That's why he leaves us sometimes. Usually he brings back seed to sow. This time he brought you instead. We are sheltered from the living here. That's all I can tell you. It is a secret's nature to remain buried. We are the secret, so we live under the earth. This village has no name. It does not exist. It lies within each one of us. When you leave here, think of yourself as a woman who has survived."

THE
MIRRORS
OF TIME

H ow do survivors walk? With their heads lowered, eyes downcast, hands behind their backs, wandering a random path until they glimpse a dimly lit house in the distance? I walked without looking back. I wanted to forget, to believe that what had happened to me was just another hallucination, a truncated dream in which everything was all mixed up: a father's burial and a freed slave's flight. I walked without speaking to anyone. Neither the children nor the men I passed bothered me. Yet I must have looked strange, badly dressed, my face haggard, wet with tears. At nightfall I curled up under a tree and wept in silence, without sadness and with no regrets. I don't think I shed a tear on the day of my father's burial.

A single sentence spoken by my mother—she who never spoke—suddenly rang in my ears. I remember I had gooseflesh when I first heard it.

It was at a time when nothing was going right. My father sensed that death was near, perhaps hastened by his persistent feeling of guilt and sin. He was bitter, irritable, impatient, and wholly without joy. Hatred, blind and violent, seethed within him. I think he hated everybody, himself first of all. Curiously, I was the only exception. I think he even loved me. I was exempt from the brutality that had become his normal mode of communication. From my bedroom window I sometimes witnessed disputes between him and the female contingent of the house. He was the only one to shout, to threaten, to laugh at his own supremacy. He had become maniacal, unable to tolerate the slightest lapse in the observation of his own rituals. Each of his daughters had an assigned role: one removed his jellaba, another washed his feet, a third dried them, and the two others made his tea. And woe betide anyone who made a mistake! Terror reigned, and he was never satisfied.

When he had an attack of bronchitis, he refused to take his medicine. When he couldn't breathe and writhed with chest pains, he accused the rest of the family of stealing his share of oxygen. He may not have even been sick, but the presence of all those useless women annoyed him so much that he was short of breath.

Rejecting sickness and death, he fought back with incredible energy. He felt a need to take his unjust violence out on his own family. He had discovered instinctively that hatred was an antidote to decay, sustaining his position as lord of the manor and warding off the progress

46

of disease. Sometimes he talked to himself, believing as he did that no one else in the house was worth speaking to. Except me. He would like to have confided in me, to have discussed his problems, but I never gave him the chance. I was hurt by the way he was acting. I understood it, but I could not excuse it or talk about it with him. In the last months of his life, I was already suffering a crisis of my own. I was fighting my own violence, determined to escape from it somehow. But as the proverb says: "It's a lot easier to enter the baths than to leave." I had to escape from that situation cleansed of the suspicions I harbored about myself, suspicions that were well justified.

My mother, who had opted for silence and resignation, out of calculation more than fatalism, said to me one day when my father's harsh words had hurt her deeply: "Pray with me, my daughter, that God or Fate let me die before you, but that I be granted just a month or two of life after your father's death! How I would love to be able to breathe for a few days or weeks in his absence. That is my sole desire, my only wish. Were I to die before him, I would go doubly battered, horribly laid waste, humiliated. I am resigned to living in silence, my voice stifled by my own hand. But may I be granted some time, however short, to utter just one scream from the depths of my soul, a scream that has lurked deep in my breast for so long, since before you were born. That scream is waiting, eating at me, ravaging me, and I want to live so that I do not die with it still inside me. Pray for me, my daughter, you who know life from both sides, you who can read both books and the hearts of saints."

I had forgotten even the sound of her voice: my mother, thrust aside by my father and by my own story. She called me "daughter" as if nothing had happened in those twenty years. I can't say that I loved her. When I wasn't feeling sorry for her—a feeling of bitter shame or mute anger—I paid no attention to her. It was as if she did not exist. I did not see her, and I forgot that she was my mother. Sometimes I mixed her up with Malika, an old servant woman, or with the ghost of a mad beggarwoman who took refuge in the entranceway of our house from time to time when children chased her, hurling stones and insults. When I came home in the evening, I would step over a body wrapped in an army blanket. I wouldn't even look to see whether it was the madwoman or my mother, thrown out of her own home. Even if I was upset, I never showed it. Just closed my eyes, so as not to see, not to hear. And most of all not to speak. What was going on inside me had to stay inside me, unseen, for there was nothing to say. Or maybe too much to say, too much to expose and denounce. I lacked the desire and the courage. Once I lost my balance on the tightrope, I felt I needed time to cast off twenty years of make-believe. If I was to be born anew, I had to wait for my father and mother to die. I considered ways to bring their deaths about, or to hasten them. I would have written that sin off to the monster I had become.

My mother sank into madness. One of her aunts took her away to live out the rest of her days in a marabout's place on the road to the South. I think she finally came to enjoy all those fake bouts of insanity, when she would tear up her husband's things. In the end she really didn't know what she was doing.

I watched her departure from my bedroom window. Her hair was tangled, her dress torn. She howled, ran around in the courtyard like a child, kissed the ground and the walls, laughed, cried, and crawled to the gate on all fours like an unwanted animal. Her daughters cried. My father wasn't there.

That night a great heaviness of silence and remorse settled over the house. We were all strangers. My sisters left to take temporary refuge with some aunts on my mother's side. I thus found myself alone with my father in his defeat.

The girls came back to get things now and then, but left without looking in on the sick man. Only old Malika remained loyal. At night she would let the mad beggar-woman in, or the coalman, who liked to chat with her. They were from the same village.

Despite the pain in his chest, my father decided to fast during Ramadan. He hardly ate anything even at sunset. He refused to take his pills, allowing himself to die in stubborn silence. I continued to go to the shop during the day. I was putting things in order. My father's brothers never came to see him. They figured that because of me, they stood to inherit nothing anyway.

I think that everything was ready on the eve of the twenty-seventh night of Ramadan.

Now it was all becoming clear. I can't say that I had decided what to do, but I knew that when my father died I would abandon everything and go away. The girls could have it all, and I would leave that house and that family forever. Once my father was gone, something else would be finished too. The monster he had created would go to the grave with him.

I lost my bearings completely after the burial. For days I did not know where I was or with whom. But I have told you of that adventure, which seemed so marvelous but ended in fear and wandering.

I went back to the house one night. I got in through a neighbor's terrace. My sisters had come back. They were well-dressed and outrageously made up; they wore my mother's jewelry. They were laughing and playing with some other neighborhood women. Burial and mourning were a liberation for them, a festival. When all is said and done, I could understand their reaction. Frustrated girls kept apart from life for so long, they were discovering freedom. All the pent-up hysteria was coming out. Every light in the house was on. They were playing records on an old phonograph. It was party time. All they needed now were men. I smiled. It was none of my business anymore: I had already become a stranger. I opened my bedroom door quietly, took a few things I had kept in a bag, and left through the same terrace.

Wearing a jellaba and a scarf I headed for the cemetery. It was a clear night. I stepped over a low wall to avoid being seen by the guard and went to my father's grave.

It was the eve of the end of Ramadan. More stars than usual. The earth covering the grave was still fresh. I dug quickly and methodically, by hand. I was careful not to disturb the dead man or to attract the guard's attention. When I saw a piece of white shroud, I slowly moved the soil away with my fingers. The body was icy, the shroud damp from the soil. I shivered, though it was not cold. I stopped for a moment and stared at the dead man's head. It looked like the white material near his nostrils was moving. Was he still breathing, or was it just a hallucination? I emptied the bag, which contained almost everything I possessed: a man's shirt, a pair of trousers, a piece

50

of a birth certificate, a photograph of the circumcision ceremony, my identity card, the marriage certificate for me and poor Fatima, the medicine I had made my father take, socks, shoes, a ring of keys, a belt, a tin of snuff, a packet of letters, an account book, a ring, a handkerchief, a broken watch, a vial, a half-burned candle.

Before filling in the grave, I squatted down to pack the objects in and felt a pain in my chest, as though something were squeezing my rib cage. My breasts were still wrapped tight to stop them from growing. In a rage I tore off the wretched disguise, several yards of white cloth. I unrolled it and wrapped it around the dead man's neck, then knotted it and pulled it tight. I was sweating. I got rid of all my life, a time of lies and deception. I tamped the objects down on the body with my hands and feet, stepping on it a little. I filled in the grave. The mound was bigger now. I covered it with heavy stones and meditated for a moment, not to pray or to ask God's mercy on that poor man's soul, but to soak up the new air I now breathed. I said, "So long." Or maybe it was "Farewell, fictive glory, and may we both live, naked and blank, the soul virginal and the body new, however old the words!"

A
DAGGER
CARESSING
MY BACK

O n that gloomy, blazing night I disappeared. I left no footsteps in the darkness. I skirted the town, choosing to skim over the countryside so as not to trouble the placid sleep of the good people in their homes. I was not one of them, for I was an uncontrollable troublemaker.

I felt happy on that September night, soaked in the fragrant whiffs of jasmine and wild roses coming from the gardens. I breathed in the scents deeply and walked down the road that lay before me. I was at peace with myself, and ready for adventure. I never looked back to see my native abyss one last time. I had entombed everything: father and possessions in the same grave, mother with a marabout at the gates of hell, sisters in a house that would someday collapse and bury them forever. My aunts and uncles had never existed for me anyway, and from that night on I did not exist for them either. I was leaving, and they would never find me.

I kept walking, avoiding the roads. When I grew tired I would stop to sleep, preferably under a tree. I slept peacefully, without fear or anxiety. My body curled up and abandoned itself to a gentle torpor. Rarely had I slept so deeply and so well. I was surprised at how easy it was, at the pleasure of feeling my body grow heavy in repose, for I had often had trouble falling asleep. I would sometimes spend most of the night bargaining for a little peace, achieving it only at first light, overcome with fatigue. But now I feared nothing. I had no bonds, no moorings. My mind was no longer encumbered with all those questions, all those things to do or undo. Completely free? No, not yet. But the very fact of having cast off everything, of having left, never to go back, of having cut myself off from all trace of the past, released my mind from fear. I was determined to dissolve my past in the coma of complete amnesia, with no regrets and no remorse. I wanted to be born anew in a fresh, clean skin.

I had no extravagant dreams or nightmares when I slept in the open air. It was a limpid sleep, smooth as the surface of a tranquil sea or a flat, continuous stretch of snow. At first I thought this was just physical tiredness, but later I realized that it was the sleep of life's first moments.

Now and then, especially during the day, I had hot waves of anxiety. They didn't last long. A lump would come to my throat, I would stop, then everything would slowly return to normal. These were the final twitches of a past that was still too close, within reach of eye and hand. That bodily discomfort was solitude's doing. I had chosen paths rarely trodden. I ate whatever I could and drank a lot of water. I asked for water whenever I passed near a hut or farmhouse. People took me for a beggar and gave me bread and fruit as well. When I tried to pay, they refused to take my money. I saw a kind of anxious pity in their eyes. I would never stay long, always leaving before the questions started. I would have liked to have stayed to talk, but I didn't know what to say. No one would have understood anyway. What's the point of having a conversation about time? But one afternoon a man followed me as I left a small village.

"But where are you going all alone, sister?" he asked, his tone somewhat ironic.

I smiled and went on my way without turning around.

"Do you realize where you're headed, sister? You are on your way to a thick wood, where wild boar wait in the dark to devour their prey. Boar with claws of bronze, with teeth of ivory and nostrils that breathe fire."

I shuddered from head to toe. I was not afraid of the man with the soft voice. I had heard talk of rapes in the forest, but had no desire to flee, or even to resist if the man turned into a boar. It was not that I didn't care. I was curious. A man whose face I did not even know was arousing physical feelings in me with words alone.

I quickened my step. We were only a few yards apart. I heard him mutter what sounded like a prayer. Nothing about wild beasts tearing at a girl's body anymore. Now the subject was God and His Prophet. This was his incantation:

"In the name of God, the Merciful, the Compassionate,

55

God's blessing and salvation upon the seal of the prophets, our master Mohammed, and upon his family and his
companions. In the name of God Most High. Praise be
to God, Who has decreed that man's greatest pleasure
lies in woman's warm insides. Praise be to God, Who has
placed in my path this nubile body advancing to the outer
limits of my desire. It is the sign of His blessing, His
bounty, His compassion. Praise be to God—and praise
be to you too, sister, for walking before me that I might
smell your perfume, imagine your hips and breasts,
dream of your eyes and hair. O sister, walk on to the
bushes where our famished bodies might dwell. Do not
turn back. I am laid open to love, with you, my unknown
sister, sent by fate to bear witness to God's glory for the
man and woman who will be joined at nightfall. Praise
be to God. I am His slave. As I am yours. The sun sinks
slowly, and with it my pride crumbles. In the name of
God, the Merciful . . ."

I stopped, as if gripped by some invisible force. I could
not go on. I looked right and left and realized that I had
gone into a copse. The man was still behind me. He had
stopped praying. I could hear his breathing. Neither of
us said a word. I stood sweating, rooted to the spot; there
were bushes everywhere. I waited for a moment. So did
he, motionless. I looked up at the sky, vivid with the
colors of the setting sun. I was suddenly very warm. I
took off my jellaba, unaware of what I was doing. Underneath I wore only a loose-fitting saroual. I untied my
hair. I stood like a statue. In a few minutes it was dark.
I felt the man coming closer to me. He was trembling,
muttering prayers. He took me by the hips. I felt his
tongue run over my neck, my shoulders. He knelt. I re-

56

mained standing. He kissed my back, his hands still on my hips. He undid my saroual with his teeth. He pressed his face, wet with sweat or tears, against my butt. He was delirious. He pulled me to the ground with a sudden movement. I let out a little cry. He put his left hand over my mouth and held me face down with the other. I had neither the strength nor the desire to resist. I was not thinking. I was free under the weight of that feverish body. For the first time another body was mingling with mine. I didn't even try to turn around to see his face. All my limbs shook. The night was black. I felt a warm, thick liquid on my thighs. The man groaned like a dying animal. I thought I heard another invocation of God and the Prophet. I slid my right hand along my belly, feeling the liquid I was losing. It was blood.

Without trying to free myself from that unknown man's grip, I let the night carry me into a deep sleep. When the fresh morning breeze awakened me, I was naked. The man was gone. I was neither unhappy nor disappointed. Was that love? A dagger caressing my back in the darkness? A scathing violence that clasps you from the rear like a random target, punctuated by prayers and incantations?

I asked myself the question, but I was not really looking for any answers. Even now I am not sure whether that encounter from the rear had caused me pleasure or disgust. I had read books that spoke of love, but not of sex. That union of two bodies left a taste of sand in my mouth. That must have been the taste and smell of love. It was not unpleasant.

There was blood on my fingers and between my legs, but I felt neither dirty nor sullied. I got dressed and went

57

on my way. Something echoed in my head, the sound of a hammer on stone or a piece of marble. It was the memory of the man's heartbeat.

My first man, then, was faceless. Had he asked me questions, it would have been unbearable. Had he not disappeared into the night, I would have fled.

I saw no one on the road that day. I had the feeling that all the people I would meet would come from the rear. It was an obsession. That evening I entered the town where I would become part of a disturbing story. It was a small town, and I felt a pang of anguish as I entered. A bad sign. First of all I looked for a public bath, both to wash and to find a place to sleep. It was late. The woman at the till glared at me.

"A fine time to come to get rid of male spit," she said.

I didn't answer.

"I was about to close," she went on, "but two or three women are still dawdling in there. Hurry up."

I hurried. She watched me. There were two impressively thin women in the back room, near the hot water fountain. They looked like twins of misfortune. Each one sat in a corner and mechanically poured cups of water over her head. They had staked out their territory with buckets. I could see that they did not want to be disturbed. From time to time they got up, stood back to back, rubbed their hands, then returned to their corners. I washed quickly. I had my head down when one of them appeared before me and said authoritatively:

"I'll soap you."

I did not look up. Her bony knees were in front of my face.

"No, thank you," I said.

"I said I'll soap you."

The other woman stood blocking the doorway with a row of buckets.

It seemed a particularly dishonest proposal, but I acquiesced to the threat. I asked if I could get some water. I filled a bucket with scalding water, hurled it at the two women, and dashed for the exit. I was lucky not to slip, and a moment later I was standing naked alongside the cashier.

"Are you crazy? You'll catch cold," she shouted at me.

"No, I'm not crazy. I barely got away. There are two of them."

"What are you talking about? There's no one here anymore. The last three left when you came in, didn't you see them go? Are you trying to fool me?"

When she saw that I was trembling—icy with fear—she hesitated for a moment, then asked me what they looked like.

"There are two of them, thin as rails and absolutely identical. They wanted to soap me!"

"You must have been dreaming. You're so tired you must have seen the devil and his wife!"

She was afraid too. She had looked mean, but now she was being very nice, though still authoritarian.

"Do you have a place to sleep?"

"I was going to ask you if I could spend the night here."

"Here? Out of the question. For one thing, it's not comfortable, and for another, the two jinn might come back late at night and scare you. A girl with such pretty skin as yours doesn't sleep just anywhere. Come to our house. It's simple, but comfortable. I live with my brother. He's younger than me."

THE
SEATED
WOMAN

To get to the house we had to go through various intersecting alleyways that seemed laid out either at random or according to the designs of some depraved builder. One, called One-person Street, was so narrow that only one person at a time could walk through. They say lovers used to meet there. They would enter from opposite ends, and when they got to the middle, they would have an excuse to touch, since there was no room to pass. The woman, veiled and in her jellaba, would put one hand across her belly, the other across her chest. When he reached her, the man would stop for a moment and feel his beloved's breath on his face. One-person Street was the hidden rendezvous of stolen kisses and caresses, the place where bodies in love could touch,

61

where eyes could plunge into a gaze unknown. Other eyes, hidden behind blinds, would watch these encounters.

Garbage was strewn on the ground. Every house had a pile of filth at the door. It stank, but no one seemed to care. A cat wailed like an unloved child. I followed the Seated Woman's large body.

"They really ought to call it Half-person Street," she said.

As she passed, she kicked a fat-bellied cat. It did not meow, but howled like a wounded man. She stopped at a door with iron bars and padlocks, then said:

"Behind this door misfortune has done its work. A sterile woman had children. A drought fell upon the country, then terrible flooding. This was misfortune's branch office. An otherwise normal man copulated with his children. One day the house collapsed on them. No one dug them out. The doors and windows were blocked up, sand and cement poured over everything. They're all still there, mother, father, and children, united forever by earth and hellfire. Misfortune seems to have eased off since then, causing no catastrophes, though it lurks here still."

I wondered why she was telling me these sinister stories. I was curious about what might happen to me, not about what had already happened behind the walls of those alleyways. But she went on, listing all the neighbors.

"In this house there's a family of no real interest. He's a tanner. Nobody dares to shake his hand, it stinks so much. And here there's a horse who lives by itself. And this one's empty, no one knows why. An abandoned house is like an unfinished story. Over there was the dairy. It's a Koranic school now. That's where the Consul gives his lessons. It's right near the house."

The house had two floors. Though not very big, it towered over the others. In the summer people lived on the terraces. The Seated Woman took me to a room furnished and decorated in traditional style. She told me to wait, not to move. I looked at the walls. Wrinkled human faces seemed to loom out of the stains of damp. They began to move as I stared at them. A portrait of an old man wearing a turban hung on the wall. He looked ill. It was a black-and-white photograph retouched with color, and everything had faded with age; the paper, the red of the lips, the blue of the turban, the tone of the skin. Time had done its work, restoring the weariness that had dwelled in that face when the photograph was first taken. It must have been the woman's father or grandfather, infinite sadness in his eyes. A man looking at the world for the last time.

The Seated Woman's voice tore me away from my thoughts.

"That was our father. He wasn't happy and neither are we. That photograph was taken not long before he died. Anyway. The Consul will see you tomorrow."

She hesitated, smiled slightly, and added:

"Or rather, you'll see him tomorrow. Let's eat something. I don't know why, but I feel at ease with you. Normally I tend not to trust people. But the moment I saw you I thought we might get along. I forgot to ask if you're looking for work, because if you are—"

"What did you have in mind?"

"Looking after the Consul."

"Is he ill?"

"He's blind. He lost his sight at the age of four, after a fever that almost killed him."

I agreed.

"You'll pick it up as you go along. I don't know anything about you, which is just as well. If you betray us, I'll come after you. I sacrificed everything for my brother . . . I am determined to have peace in this house."

I looked around as she spoke, thinking of my father. I saw him standing at the door, lecturing my mother. It was her sharp tone that reminded me of my father.

Some people shout when they feel threatened, their feelings darkened by anger. Others speak without raising their voice, and their words have greater effect. The Seated Woman was quite capable of doing what she said.

Dark and strong, with an impressive rear end—hence her name—she seemed ageless. A smooth, matt face. Her corpulence was an advantage, not a handicap, in her job. Her strategic position at the baths must have been the envy of the intelligence service. She knew everything, including all the neighborhood families; she got involved in various intrigues, helped arrange marriages, set up meetings. She was the neighborhood's registry and memory, a woman of secrets and trust, fear and tenderness. She kept an eye on everyone who came in, looked after everything, kept the fire going in the oven near the baths. She had big breasts that frightened children, but adolescents dreamed of burying their heads in all that weight. Usually unmarried, often widowed or divorced, a Seated Woman has no real family life of her own. She stands apart, and no one is interested in how—or with what jinni—she spends her nights. People make up an imaginary life for her, making her incestuous or homosexual,

64

a fortuneteller or a caster of spells, a monster or a pervert.

There was a time when the Seated Woman, who now could barely climb a flight of stairs, had youth, a lover, maybe even a husband. She had had a dowry, a house, jewelry. She must have been slim, perhaps even beautiful. I looked at her fat, tired body and tried to discern the picture of the girl she had been before everything had been turned upside down in a matter of seconds. Everybody had perished in the earthquake, and she stood in the ruins with her traumatized little brother, his eyes unseeing forever after.

She told me the story one night when we couldn't sleep. The Consul was snoring and we lay waiting for morning, when we would go for mint for the tea and fritters. She told me nothing about her life before the catastrophe. I liked to imagine her happy, with a house, a home, a man. Perhaps she had not been there in Agadir that night, but somewhere else, with a husband who beat her and slept with other women. Perhaps he left with a niece or a cousin, going far away, leaving the country, never to be heard from again.

I said nothing. I sometimes glimpsed traces of humiliation in her eyes.

"Yes, I was abandoned, thrown into the street, and as the proverb says, 'No cat flees a house where there's a wedding.' If he left, he must have had a reason. 'Do you know how to hold on to a man?' my mother used to say. 'With this and this,' one hand on her belly, and the other on her butt. 'But who wants a body that's been used and abused like yours? No one, or everyone. Who wants a divorcée who's still married, a widow with no corpse or inheritance, a wife without a home? I bear that burden, like a mountain on my chest. What am I supposed to say to my cousins and neighbors? That my daughter didn't give her husband pleasure, so he looked elsewhere for what he couldn't find in his marriage bed? No, it's too much.' "

She must have gone away to escape such reproach, to cease to be the woman abandoned, marked for insult and contempt. Her younger brother must have followed her, clinging to her jellaba, crying and begging. Their wanderings must have been hard. Hunger, cold, and illness. The kid probably went blind from trachoma. She did laundry for rich families, sometimes cooked for weddings or baptisms, raised her brother as if he were her own son. She wanted a better life for him, fought to get him a state scholarship. He became a schoolteacher and gave neighborhood children lessons in the Koran.

She had wanted him to be a minister or ambassador, but he was only a consul in an imaginary city in a ghost country. It was she who named him to this job. He went along with it because he "didn't want to hurt her," as he told me later. She was pleased and he never crossed her. That was the deal. The unspoken conventions of their daily ritual made this brother and sister a strange and dubious couple. Reality was masked by a theatrical game.

At first I thought they were just having fun, or trying to entertain me. They were sometimes tyrannical, sometimes romantically effusive. They spoke in flowery language even when shouting at each other. The most important ritual took place in the morning. The Seated Woman would wake the Consul up by singing softly, murmuring verses as she approached his door:

My gazelle, my heart,
My beauty, my prince,
Light of my eyes,
Open your arms . . .

She took her time, always waking him up gently. She often brought him flowers and he always asked first about their color, not their scent. He would touch one and say, "The red is too bright" or "That yellow feels nice."

She would kiss his hand. If he did not pull it away, that meant that he was in a good mood and she would have his blessing for the day. Then they would shut themselves up in the bathroom together and she would shave him, perfume him, and dress him. Then they would go out, his hand resting on hers. They walked slowly, waving to an imaginary crowd.

At first I had to make an effort not to laugh. Later I learned to play the game, standing in for the huge crowd that rose early to greet the princely couple.

I was sitting on a stool at the low table where breakfast was served when I heard him say in the corridor:

"I feel there is a flower in the house. It needs water. Why didn't you tell me?"

I rose to greet the Consul when they came in. He held out his hand for me to kiss it. I shook it and sat down again.

"A flower, but a rebellious one," he said.

I smiled. The Seated Woman signaled me to get up, as if to say, "We don't eat at the same table as the Consul."

She and I had breakfast in the kitchen, in silence.

"This house is all we have," she told me. "I have to

run it and protect it from indecent, jealous eyes. I look after everything. I have to think of everything, and most of all make sure the Consul lacks for nothing. We make enough to live on. Sometimes I have to stay late at the baths, and I think of the Consul. When he gets bored, he turns on the radio. It means he's annoyed. I can't stand having to be a man at the baths and a woman at home, sometimes even both at once in both places. You're going to have to help me. The Consul needs someone to reassure him when I'm not here. He likes someone to read to him in the evenings. But I can't read, so I make up stories. If he doesn't like them he gets annoyed, thinks I'm treating him like a child. I don't know any more stories. Lately he's been getting impatient, irritable, even nasty. I can't stand it. I need help. The schedule is the same every weekday: the Koranic school in the morning, a siesta in the afternoon. In the evening he's free. You will take care of him in the evening."

THE
CONSUL

I was overcome by a strange drowsiness during the first week. It was as if I was somewhere else. I slept without dreaming. I would get up and wander around the house for hours, alone with those quaint old objects, the threadbare carpets and the father's photograph over the cupboard. I stared at that photograph until my eyes clouded over. I loved the idleness and solitude, and not having to answer to anyone. I was wide awake by the time the Consul came home in the evening. During the day time stretched into a hammock on which I could lie down and daydream. I would stare wide-eyed at the winding shapes drawn by the damp patches on the ceiling. The past swept over me, image by image. I could not resist the reckless arrival of so many memories. They were all the same sepia color. Voices, shouts, and sighs came with them in a procession in which I saw myself as a child, but not as all the others had made me.

There was a room at the back of our big house, a kind of granary where they kept supplies of wheat, oil, and olives for the winter. A windowless room, dark and cold, ruled by mice and fear. My father locked me in there once. I can't remember why. I trembled with cold and fury. Now I could not shake off the memory of that inhospitable room. From the depths of my hammock I called up my father, my mother, my seven sisters, signaling them to come into the room. I locked the door, sprinkled oil around, and set fire to it. I had to start over several times, for the damp and the draught blew out the flames. The fire blazed around my family but did not touch them. They stood together through the ordeal, waiting motionless for the joke to end.

I drove away that image with a wave of my hand and tried to think about something else. But all my visions were sinister.

A narrow, deserted street; with stones growing out of the wall like dried pomegranates. Pieces of words, obscene drawings, and graffiti were written on the whitewashed smooth parts. Parents avoided the place when they had their children with them. It was in that street, no wider than a grave, that I met my father. I stood face to face with him, not looking at the sky, but trying to decipher the words and drawings on the wall. I didn't speak to him. I read out loud what was written on the wall: "Love is a snake slithering between thighs" . . .

"Balls are tender apples" . . . "My cock rises before the sun." My father, with his back to the wall, was standing with his head between two parted thighs. I pushed him aside and saw a graphic drawing of a vagina with teeth. Above it someone had written: "The teeth of pleasure." There was a front view of a body, its sex the only clear feature; on the tip was a skull: the entire body was a penis, walking, smiling, impatient. Around the drawing were innumerable names for the female sex organ: door, blessing, slit, mercy, beggar, lodging, storm, spring, oven, tent, warmth, dome, madness, delight, joy, valley, rebel . . . I called them out one by one, yelling them in my father's ear as he stood pale, his face showing no expression. I shook him as if to wake him up. He was cold and pallid, long dead.

That narrow street, the street of shame, led to the abyss. I was curious. I wanted to follow it to the end. The street had been abandoned by its inhabitants, for rumor had it that it led to hell, that it ended at a courtyard where the heads of the dead were laid out like watermelons. No one ever went down it anymore. A street damned, where dead men from hell took refuge now and then.

I had assumed that my father, despite his prayers and his almsgiving, would spend some time in hell. Now I was sure. He must have been paying for his sins. I will probably join him one day, since I am the main source of his sins. But before that I have to live.

I was deep in these thoughts when I saw the Consul going into the kitchen. I got up. He waved at me to sit back down. I stayed put. He made some mint tea. His hands knew where everything was. They didn't hesitate or feel around, but went straight to each object. When the teapot was ready, he said:

"Could you please boil some water?"

He never touched the stove. When the water boiled, he poured it into the teapot. He turned off the gas and let the tea steep. He sat down and said:

"This tea won't be very good. I apologize. The mint is not fresh. Someone forgot to buy more. You may serve it now."

We drank in silence. The Consul seemed pleased.

"It isn't really teatime," he said, "but I felt like having some anyway. I hope I'm not disturbing you. I could have had it sent in from the café on the corner, but I wanted to make it here."

I didn't know what to say.

"Why are you blushing?" he asked.

I put my hands to my cheeks. They were warm. I was impressed by the elegance and grace of his gestures. I dared not look at him. He seemed to have a sixth sense that allowed him to know everything. I moved back a little and watched him. I'm not really sure whether he was handsome, but he had presence. No, it was something more than that. He was intimidating.

He got up when he finished his tea.

"I have to go," he said. "The kids are terrible. I try to teach them the Koran as I would a beautiful poem, but they keep asking awkward questions, like, 'Is it true that all the Christians will go to hell?' or 'Since Islam is the best religion, why did God wait so long to spread it?' I merely look up at the ceiling and repeat the question:

'Why was Islam so late in coming?' Do you have any idea what the answer is?"

"I've thought about it. But I'm like you, I like the Koran as an exquisite poem, and I detest people who exploit it like parasites and limit freedom of thought. They're hypocrites. In fact, the Koran itself mentions them."

"Yes, I see what you mean."

After a brief silence he quoted verse 2 of the sura "The Hypocrites":

" 'They have made for themselves a veil of their oaths. They have barred men from the ways of salvation. Surely their deeds are marked in the corner of iniquity.' Fanatical believers or hypocrites, what's the difference? To me they're alike. I like to stay away from both."

"I know them well. I've run into them before. They invoke religion to crush and to dominate. For myself, I invoke the right of free thought, the right to believe or not to believe. It's nobody's business but my own. I have negotiated my freedom with the night and its ghosts."

"I like it when you smile."

It was true that the hint of a smile crossed my face when I spoke of the night. He asked me to lend him a clean handkerchief. He took off his dark glasses and wiped them meticulously. On his way out, he stopped in front of the mirror, adjusted his jellaba, and combed his hair.

I straightened up the house and shut myself up in the bathroom. There was no sink or tub, just bowls placed under cold-water taps. I looked at myself in a small mirror. I had lost weight. My breasts were sticking out. I put my hands between my thighs. It still hurt. I was no longer a virgin. The encounter in the wood had been brutal and blind. There was no feeling or judgment in the memory. It was one adventure among so many others I had had. Things would cross my body without leaving wounds. I had decided all that quite calmly. I was teaching myself to forget, to not look back. I had to drive out the horde of memories that pursued me, each more shameful, execrable, and unbearable than the next. I knew that I would be plagued by that bundle of knotted rope for some time to come. The only escape was not to be there when they knocked at the door of my sleep. So I decided to look after the house and the Consul seriously, to become a woman, to be sensitive to everything, and to regain for my body the gentleness that had been taken from it.

The Consul's room was lit by two windows. It was clean, neat, and pleasant, tastefully decorated. There was a mixture of colors in the fabrics, and a Berber carpet brought brightness and warmth. A small bookcase contained books in braille. At the bedside was an alarm clock, a photograph of the Consul and his sister, an ashtray, a pitcher of water, and a glass. At the back of the room was a table with a typewriter, a half-typed page in the machine. I resisted the temptation to read even the first line, but I was curious. I moved away, then tried to make out a few words. From the page layout I decided it must have been a private journal. On the table was a red folder containing a packet of paper. I blushed. I was ashamed and annoyed at myself for having discovered the secret. The Consul was keeping a journal, probably unknown to his sister.

The first incident took place that evening. The Seated Woman arrived carrying provisions for dinner and went straight to the kitchen. On her way in she noticed the teapot, still full of mint, and the two glasses, which I had forgotten to rinse. She put down her basket and asked me whether someone had come to visit during the day. I told her no one had come.

"Who had tea, then?"

"The Consul and I."

"The Consul never drinks tea at home during the day."

"He does. He made it himself this morning. Ask him and he'll tell you."

"No. He's working in his room. He mustn't be disturbed. Was the tea good?"

"Yes, not too sweet, the way I like it."

From his room the Consul commented: "The tea was good, but the time spent with our Guest was even better."

The Seated Woman said nothing. She was in a bad mood. I offered to help her. She said no and asked me to go and wash the Consul's feet.

"It's time. Heat some water and get the towel and perfume ready."

I had never washed a man's feet before. The Consul sat in an armchair and held out his right foot, while the left soaked in the warm water. I didn't do the massage very well. With no irritation, he took my hand.

"Don't rub or squeeze. Massage is somewhere between the two, a caress that goes through the skin and circulates inside."

After the lesson, I got down on my knees again and tried to get the feel of it. His feet were not big. I massaged them slowly. He was obviously pleased. He smiled and muttered "Allah, Allah," an exclamation of pleasure.

Dinner went well. The sister was tired.

"You'll read to him tonight," she said.

"No, not tonight," the Consul said. "I want to continue the discussion I was having with our Guest this morning."

He asked me to follow him out to the terrace.

"The nights are mild and lovely out there, especially now, as summer slowly ends. And I like it when the sky's so starry. In two days the moon will be full. You'll see how beautiful it is."

There was a carpet, and two cushions lay on the ground. The town was still awake. There were people on the terraces, eating dinner or playing cards. I was watching them when he told me to look closely at the third terrace on the right.

"Are they out there?"

"Who?"

"A man and a woman, young, not married. They often meet on the terrace to make love. They kiss, put their arms around each other, and whisper sweet words back and forth. I come here when I'm lonely, and I know they'll keep me company. They can't see me. And I can't see them either. But I can feel them, and I like them. They steal a few hours of happiness, and I'm glad to be a discreet witness to that happiness. Sometimes I live by proxy, you know. That's all right, but I shouldn't let it happen too often. Anyway, I won't bore you with all my little stories. What were we talking about this morning?"

"Islam."

"Islam! Perhaps we are unworthy of the nobility of that religion?"

"Isn't every religion based on guilt? I have renounced the world, withdrawn from it in the mystical sense, rather like al-Hallaj."

"I don't quite understand."

"I have broken with the world, or at least with my past. Thrown it all away, deliberately cut myself loose. I am trying to be happy, to live according to my needs, with my own body. I have torn out the roots and the masks. I am a wanderer, held back by no religion. I cross from myth to myth, indifferent."

"That's what you call freedom."

"Yes, to cast off everything, to own nothing so as not to be owned. To be free of all shackles, perhaps even of time itself."

"You remind me of that Zen phrase, 'In the beginning man has nothing.' "

"Man has nothing in the beginning, that's true, and he ought to have nothing at the end either. But he is inculcated with the need to possess: a house, parents, children, stones, deeds, money, gold, people. I am learning to possess nothing."

"That thirst for possession and consumption is the expression of a great lack within us. Something essential is missing. We don't even know what it is. I once knew a great gentleman who lived with his hands in his pockets, no house, no baggage, no ties. He died as he was born, with nothing. He was a poet, and a man of his word."

"To possess, to accumulate, to save up for things—doesn't it amount to risking our dignity a little more each day, testing it?"

As we talked, the Consul methodically chopped some dried marijuana leaves on a board designed for the purpose. I paid no attention at first. His hands moved with patience and skill. He filled a pipe, lit it, inhaled deeply, then tapped out the ash. "Good," he said, as if talking

77

to himself. He filled a second pipe and handed it to me.

"I don't know if you'll like it," he said. "I think it's good quality. I smoke a pipe or two now and then. It helps me to figure things out, to see clearly into myself. No pun intended."

In my previous existence I had sometimes smoked kif. I didn't enjoy it much, but that night everything was good, even the kif. I felt secure. I had only just come out of hell.

The man whose feet I was learning to wash every night was not my master, and I was not his slave. We were already close to each other. I forgot his blindness and talked to him like an old friend. One evening on the terrace he commented on that:

"We get along so well, we probably have a like wound hidden within us. I don't mean the same infirmity—the blind are aggressive and mean to one another—but some broken thing inside that brings us together."

Having decided to bury my past for good, I did not answer. I was already grateful that the Consul had never tried to find out anything about my previous life. How could I tell him that my life was just beginning, that a thick curtain had been drawn over a stage on which people and objects were covered with the dust of oblivion? I was struggling silently, never letting anything show, to escape from that unhealthy labyrinth once and for all. I was fighting against guilt, religion, morality, and all the things that threatened to rise again to compromise me, sully me, betray me, destroy what little I sought to preserve deep within myself.

My encounter with the Consul was a real blessing for me, despite the minor difficulties that cropped up in everyday life. The man had built a world of his own in which he lived at his own pace. He had his habits, a ritual that might seem ridiculous or demented. It was all sustained by his sister, who thereby exercised her own power. I was not sure where I stood. Hired by chance, I did not yet know what my real job would be. The Seated Woman had told me vaguely what had to be done. But he had said nothing. I was not quite at his beck and call, but I was supposed to be available at all times. In general I like to know where I stand. In this case I was in the dark, but I liked it. The three of us seemed lost in a fog.

One evening after dinner, the Consul said to his sister in an authoritative tone:

"Tomorrow you will clean up the baths. I've decided that all three of us will go for a wash."

"But that isn't possible!"

"It will be. The baths will be reserved for the family tomorrow. We will all go, you, our Guest, and I . . ."

"But—"

"There is nothing to fear. I can't very well intrude on your privacy."

I said nothing. I felt that the Seated Woman was relying on me to help her block his plan. In fact, I was intrigued and pleased at the idea of all of us washing together like a family.

"Very well, then," his sister said. "The last customers leave about nine o'clock. Come before ten."

She got up and went to her room. The Consul seemed content, though a little worried.

"I don't like to see my sister angry," he said. "She probably thinks I'm doing this to spite her. I do have strange ideas from time to time. I get that way when I'm

79

nervous. I didn't ask your opinion. Would you mind if—"

"We'll see tomorrow!"

"I say that because you're a woman; in fact, as far as I can tell, you are very feminine. So maybe finding yourself in the steamy dark with a man . . ."

"You're right. I don't want your sister to think it was my idea, that it's a kind of plot against her."

THE
PACT

O nly the main room of the baths had any light at all; the other two were dark, with a kind of half-light in which good vision might barely tell white thread from black. If the ambiguity of the soul had light, it would be that one and none other. The naked bodies were dressed in steam. The dampness ran down the walls in gray droplets, feeding on the room's endless chatter. The baths had been emptied of customers and cleaned, and we had them to ourselves. The Seated Woman, mistress of the place, entered first, holding the Consul by the hand. I followed wordlessly. I remembered my arrival here two months before, when I barely had time to wash, hurried by the Seated Woman and tormented by two witches. I walked around slowly, examining the walls. In the back room I saw a ghost, the body of a girl hanging from the ceiling. The body grew older as I came near, until I was face to face with my toothless mother, tufts of her hair strewn over her face and neck. I recoiled in horror and rejoined the Consul and his sister in the middle room. I was convinced that my memories fed on the blood of the dead, pouring it into mine. The mixture brought on hallucinations in which dry bodies demanded their blood back. I decided not to tell anyone about it. I had been haunted by that mixed-blood story ever since my father's death. My effort to forget was making some progress, for I had managed to bury some people and things. Steambaths generally lend themselves to visions. Jinn come in at night to hold their secret conversations. Early in the morning, when the doors open, there is a smell of death, and the floor is covered with peanut shells. It is well known that ghosts eat while they talk. But what I saw when I came into the middle room was no vision: the sister, a towel around her waist, was sitting astride the Consul, who lay face down. She was giving him a massage, stretching his limbs, her movements accompanied by little cries that sounded like stifled kisses. It was strange to see them in that position and to hear the Consul saying "Allah, Allah," just as he did when I washed his feet. A little smack on the bottom and the Consul changed position. He who was so slim and tall was now entirely enveloped, intertwined in the Seated Woman's fat, heavy body. They were both clearly enjoying it. I left them to their exercises and went back to the cooler entrance room. I had wrapped a fairly large towel around my waist and had begun washing my hair when the Seated Woman, grotesque in her nakedness, appeared before me and ordered me to join them.

"You have nothing to hide. What you have, I have, and my brother can't see. So relax and come with us!"

I thought it was an order from the Consul. I rinsed my hair and joined them. They were sitting in the middle room, legs apart, eating hard-boiled eggs and red olives. Which was traditional. She offered me an egg. It wasn't hard-boiled, and the yoke trickled between my fingers. I began to feel sick. For a moment I felt as if I had become the plaything of a diabolical couple, a feeling that was intensified when the Seated Woman asked me to soap her back and buttocks. The Consul giggled. She looked ridiculous with her butt in the air. I felt like I was washing a dead mountain. She fell asleep and started snoring. The Consul put his hand on my left breast, then apologized. He had meant to touch my shoulder. He asked me to let him sleep. His body was slim. His sex was erect under the towel. I kept my distance, as he could tell from the sound of my voice. He was very good at measuring distances by people's voices. He said he was happy to be in the baths with me. I told him the egg had made me sick. I got up, rushed to a corner, and threw up. The Consul was obviously sexually aroused by the atmosphere of half-darkness, steam, and dampness, coupled with the presence of two women. It was then that I realized that the fantasies of the blind were based not on images, but on smells, on particular, staged-managed situations. The Consul had withdrawn to a dark corner, his face against the wall. I knew that if I let him touch me he would lose control. He asked me quietly to soap his back. I refused.

He didn't insist. I felt no desire. Simply looking at the Seated Woman lying in the middle of the baths made me feel sick again. I washed quickly and went out to the room to rest. I fell asleep.

Was I dreaming or was I still in the baths? I heard languorous cries, followed by groans. Then I saw—at least I think I saw—the Consul curled up in his sister's arms. He was sucking her breast like a baby. I couldn't tell which of them was moaning with pleasure. It lasted for quite a while. I watched them, but they couldn't see me. Was this possible? A man so sensitive, so intelligent, reduced to infancy in that woman's arms! She massaged his feet and legs as he sucked.

When I saw them coming out, each wrapped in a large towel, I realized that they were bound by a secret, lifelong pact. They were happy and rested. Perhaps the Consul wanted to initiate me into their secret, to have me share the complicity that bound them. He seemed vexed when his sister told him that I had left the room. I thought he would have sensed it, but all his senses were occupied in his body's diversion. I knew that the blind were very touchy. The Consul was trying to control his anger. And far from losing interest in his moods, I too was affected by what had just happened. The Consul did not sleep that night. I heard him typing. The Seated Woman snored placidly, and I waited for morning. More than once I desperately wanted to go into his room, sit in a corner, and watch him write. But I was afraid of how he would react. He was annoyed, probably because of my behavior. I was troubled. My emotions were contradictory: panic mingled with a strange joy. Something had snapped in the underlying balance of our relations, which had, of course, been ambiguous but frank, marked by the promises of time and the courtesy of feelings yet undefined. But flashes of sudden, unchained passion were something else again. There may have been passion between us, but it had been halting, still in its infancy.

The only passion I had ever known was what I felt for my father, and I had carried that to its outermost limits, to hatred, death, and even hatred after death. It had destroyed everything. Unhappiness is the very essence of any passion, its kernel, motor force, and reason. You never realize this at first. It is only later, when the squall has passed, that you find out that unhappiness has been burrowing away too. That was why I was moving cautiously and fearfully. I had decided to remain a passive observer. I had to sweep out my consciousness, take the time to slough off skin and to extinguish memories forever. I pretended to have a sore throat and stayed in my room to sleep. I wanted to wait a few days before talking to the Consul again. I felt that it would be difficult to face him. He noticed everything. He was aware of the slightest shifts in the soul of anyone he was interested in.

One day when I was still in bed, he knocked at my door and proposed that we meet on the terrace at dusk. He said it was a beautiful day, with a very soft light. Ideal weather for talking. "I would love to," I said, without opening the door.

I was telling the truth. Joy filled my heart. We hadn't spoken for about ten days. Things were slowly getting back to normal. The Seated Woman was sulking. She left all the housework for me. This was her way of reminding me that I was just a servant, a housekeeper. But the Consul had treated me differently from the very beginning. I was neither a maid nor a nurse. The Seated Woman was trying to come between the Consul and me with her wretched tricks. She put a mattress in a corner of the kitchen and told me that I should sleep there from now on. I didn't protest. It was her house. I didn't care whether I slept among cooking pots, in the open air, or in a comfortable bedroom. I had no baggage to move. I slept in the kitchen and had a wonderful dream. There was a journey in it, and a boat, and I swam in pure water.

Next morning I heard an argument between the Seated Woman and her brother. It was short, but sharp. Was it a scene in the script, or just one of the blind man's fits of anger when one of his idiosyncrasies was violated? Maybe he was chiding his sister for having exiled me to the kitchen. I did not want to know. I had no business interfering in their little scenes. I said nothing, believing as I did that the attention the Consul showed me was quite enough. I was, after all, only a stranger, a vagabond with no papers, no identity, and no baggage, coming from nothingness and heading for the unknown. I was glad that they had taken me in during those first days of my wanderings. My meeting with that complex, cultured, and intimidating man was increasingly becoming a major event in my life.

I would wash the dishes and clean up the kitchen before going to bed. Cockroaches and ants kept me company. Maids usually sleep in the kitchen, even in rich families.

But this did not last long. One evening the Consul asked me to go back to my room. I refused. He insisted.

"It's an order," he said.

"Your sister . . ."

"Yes, I know. I've spoken to her about it. She's sorry.

86

Her rheumatism is acting up and she's in a bad mood."

"I take my orders from her. She's the one who brought me here, and she's the one who'll have to tell me what my new position in this house is."

"You're right. But sometimes right has to be ignored. I'm asking you."

Then, after a silence during which I felt that he was searching for the words to convey something serious, he added:

"I don't like it when you're far away, in this room that smells of grease."

At that moment the Seated Woman came in, looking tired, her hair undone.

"He's right," she said. "Don't stay in this room."

Then she left.

On the terrace was a small table, a marijuana pipe, a teapot, and two glasses. He asked me to keep him company, and he talked for most of the night.

"I have seen fabulous countries where the trees leaned over give me shade, where it rained crystals, where birds of all colors flew ahead of me to show me the way, where the wind brought me perfume. Countries with transparent ground, where I spent hours and days alone. There I met lighthearted prophets, childhood friends I had lost track of, girls I was in love with when I was small. I wandered in an exotic garden with no wall or guard. I walked on waterlilies as big as carpets. I slept undisturbed on a bench. It was a good sleep, heavy, deep, and restful. I wasn't worried in the least. I was at peace with myself and with others. But the others had been expelled from those countries. That's why I found them fabulous. People passed by in a hurry, without stopping. I walked slowly, astonished at the magnificent colors of the sky at dusk. I noticed that everybody was going in the same direction. I followed them, partly out of curiosity, but also because I had nothing special to do. They all stopped at an enormous warehouse on the edge of town. There were no houses, trees, or meadows anywhere around. The warehouse, painted blue, rose in the middle of a huge, dry field. You went in one door and came out another, your arms filled with small parcels. It was strange. I joined the line with everyone else, not really knowing why. It was remarkable how well behaved people were. As you know, civic spirit is rare among us. When I got to the entrance, I saw huge signs over large shelves. Each sign bore a letter of the alphabet. The warehouse was a word depository. The town dictionary. People came to pick up words and even sentences they might need during the week. Not just mutes and stutterers; there were also others known for having nothing to say, who repeated themselves without realizing it. And there were chatterboxes fresh out of words; and others who had a word on the tip of their tongue and looked in mirrors to find that word. Some had their meanings wrong and went to the wrong shelf. Guides took them in hand. Others liked to mix up syllables, claiming to be inventing a new language. The warehouse was like a simmering pot. I wandered through the corridors. Words were piled up, covered with a layer of dust. Nobody used them. They were piled to the ceiling. I told myself that they were either words people did not need anymore or ones they had adequate supplies of at home. I left through a service exit hidden in the wall among shelves containing broken, ruined words and very old ones that nobody used anymore. I'll let you guess what those words were, just as I'll say nothing about the vulgar words stacked in a dark corner and covered with a bright red veil.

"When I opened the door, I found myself in a huge, well-lit cellar where brunettes, blondes, and redheads walked around, all young women, each representing a particular type of beauty, a particular country, a race, or sensibility. They walked back and forth but did not speak. Some sat and dozed. Others were all excited, boasting about the product they bore within them. That huge underground expanse was the town library. A superb creature came over to me and began to speak: 'At twenty-two, I have just finished my studies at Göttingen University. My father's intention was that I travel in Europe's most remarkable countries.' And after another pause: 'I am *Adolphe*. Take me, I'm a love story. Without a happy ending, but that's life.' Naturally I thought of that story about the country where all the books had been burned and rebel citizens would each learn a book by heart to preserve literature and poetry. But this was different. Here books were not forbidden or burned, but some firm had hired pretty women to learn a novel, short story, or play by heart. For a fee, they would come to your home to be read, or more precisely, to recite the book they had learned. It must have been a black market. I had to buy a ticket to get in. A woman of some years sat on a sofa. She was not beautiful, but there was something strangely attractive about her. I went over to her, and she said, 'I am *Risalat al-Ghufran*, the Epistle of Forgiveness, a most important book, which few have actually read. I was written in 1033; my creator was born in Ma'rat al-Nu'man, near Aleppo, in northern Syria. I am a difficult book, in

89

which the dead converse, arguments are settled through poetic diatribes, and the sojourn in paradise is longer than the sojourn in hell.' It was a very lively human library. There was even a very young girl swinging on a trapeze and reciting *Ulysses*: 'Better not stick here all night like a limpet. This weather makes you dull. Must be getting on for nine by the light.' In a room decorated in the oriental style, a dozen beautiful women, all dressed as Scheherazade, each offered to tell part of the *Thousand and One Nights*. It was just like a fairy tale. It was a wonderful country, and that library was a marvel. An old man dressed in white whispered to me as he left: 'It's a sacrilege to call yourself a work of literature, to pretend to be Taha Hussein's *Days*, or Balzac's *La comédie humaine*. What nerve! Myself, I'm just a poor reader of the Koran. Can you imagine the heresy if I claimed to be the Holy Book? As well give up the keys to the world and sink into complete madness. That said, if you need someone to read a few verses over your relatives' graves, I'm your man.' A fabulous country, a country lit by the light of my sleepless nights. I get sad when I leave it. I miss it whenever I open my eyes to eternal darkness. But will and desire alone are not enough to open the gates to that country for me. I have to be in a state of grace, a particular mood. Actually, it's the country that comes to me, that visits me, with its gardens, palaces, and underground corridors teeming with life fantastic. It is my secret, my happiness. But I confess that all those mirages sometimes tire me. Their unreal beauty plagues me. But that's life. Since you've been here in the house, I feel less need to lose myself in the labyrinths of that shifting land. Are you perhaps a native of that country? I have wondered about that, because of the scent of your presence. Not the kind of scent that comes out of a bottle, but the kind that emanates from your skin, the unmistakable scent of a human being. I have a special gift for detecting that. Excuse me. I have talked too long. I must have tried your patience. Maybe you're sleepy. We didn't even drink the tea, but it is cold now. Good night!"

I fell asleep easily and dreamed of the magic country. Everything was dazzlingly bright, but I couldn't find my way to the library.

A
SOUL
DEFEATED

A t first I didn't notice—or rather did not want to see—that the Seated Woman's face was ravaged by hate. Self-hatred more than hatred of others. But it was hard to see it. Traces of more than one defeat were evident on that face, especially when she slept. The devastation was not a mask, but daily pain. Hatred alone protected that woman from physical degeneration and kept death at bay; death that would have come from immense despair.

One evening after dinner, as the Consul sat typing, the Seated Woman asked me to join her on the terrace for tea.

"Tea keeps me from sleeping," I told her.

"Then I'll make you a vervain, but it's what I have to tell you will keep you awake."

"What do you have to tell me?"

"Don't be afraid! I'm going to tell you who I am. That's all. And when you find out who lives behind this face you may not be able to sleep."

Then she did just what the Consul had done: prepared the kif, smoked two or three pipes, and began to talk. I drank my vervain and listened, at first by constraint, but then because it was so terrible. She spoke faster than usual, and sometimes paused for long silences.

"I was probably born by accident," she said. "I was ugly from the start and I stayed ugly. I used to hear people say, 'This kid has no business being here.' 'This kid is a child of drought.' I was always in the way, never at ease. No one wanted my misshapen body around. Wherever I went I saw desolation and disappointment on people's faces, especially the grown-ups.

"From the very beginning the other children kept me out of their games. Nobody wanted anything to do with this graceless face. I understood the people who were disturbed by my presence. My parents were unhappy. They wore defeat on their faces; and I was their own defeat. To banish the curse, they had a second child. When my brother was born, they had a big party. For them it was the end of the drought. But my poor brother got measles and went blind. Misfortune dogged the family. I felt responsible. That child had brought light and grace to a house without laughter, but in just a few days he was deprived of light forever. For the first time I let tears flow down my cheeks. My heart was broken, but not my face, which was expressionless, as always. With

94

that misfortune, which I considered greater than my own, I came to realize that I was born of loss. I had fallen like an evil, unexpected rain, the kind that arouses fear because it rots the seed.

"My face is like a watercolor smeared by a rag, all out of shape. Everything is askew, both the body and what's inside it. I am so filled with hate that it would take at least two lifetimes to spill it all out. But hatred does not really suit me, for if you want to hate, you also have to love, even if only a little. And I don't love anyone, not even myself. What I feel for the Consul is beyond love. It's the air I breathe, the beating of my heart. But that's unlivable. You show up in the house, and that's all it takes to make him smile again. Before you came, we couldn't even breathe here. He had even become aggressive, violent and unfair. That's why I asked you to come and live with us the moment I saw you, lost and unattached. I don't have to tell you that; you know it very well. Your presence has brought a little light into this house. You are innocent, but I am not.

"I let my parents die. I don't think anyone even went to their funerals. I left with my brother, took a few valuables, and left my parents with a mad old woman. I left without looking back, without a single tear. I emptied my life of everything that might resemble hope. And since then I've turned in a circle, sitting all the while. My brother grew up in my arms. I became his eyes. I worked hard so that he would lack for nothing. I'm afraid of losing him. I want you to help me not to lose him. I can feel misfortune coming, and I have no way to fight it. But I can see it in the distance. And I can see a silhouette, perhaps a man, but more like a woman disguised as a

95

man, walking down the road alone in a garish twilight. And I sense that that shadow can keep the misfortune away. I'm not a seer, but sometimes I have premonitions so powerful that everything becomes clear. The silhouette looks like you. Fate sent you to us, though we do not know who you are, where you come from, or what's in your mind. The Consul seems happy with you, and your presence has clearly been good for him. I have to keep you here, because you have restored my brother's desire to smile and to write. It's been months since he worked at his typewriter. I don't know what he's writing, but it must be important. If he asks you to go with him to what he calls 'the perfumed meadow,' don't be shocked, and most of all don't refuse. He goes there about once a month. I used to go with him, but now he doesn't want to be seen with me. He's ashamed of his sister who spends her life sitting at the entrance to the baths. I am not the keeper of secrets anymore. I keep old clothes, that's all. Nothing to be proud of. The job I do is ill-regarded. What did you do before you came here?"

She stopped for a moment, stuffed a pipe with kif, held it out to me, and said:

"Take some and you'll speak. It helps. Frees your mind."

I smoked some. I felt sick and coughed when I inhaled. Her eyes were anxious and impatient.

"I want to know," she said. "Tell me! Who are you? What miraculous thing do you carry inside you? How have you managed to bring a dying man back to life?"

She began to sob and weep. It was a grotesque situation, and I decided to say a few words to end it.

"Before I came to this town, it was my privilege and

96

good fortune to bathe in a spring of exceptional qualities. One of them—the ability to wipe out memories—is vital to me. The waters of that spring cleansed me, body and soul, wiping my memories clean and reordering what little remains of my past, three or four memories. Everything else is gone, and in their place I see only ruins and fog. My past is wrapped in a worn woolen blanket. To gain access to that spring you have to cast off everything and renounce nostalgia forever. I destroyed my identity papers and followed the star that traced the route of my destiny. That star follows me everywhere. I can show it to you if you want. The day it flickers out will be the day of my death. I have forgotten everything: childhood, parents, my family name. When I see myself in a mirror, I realize that I am happy, because even that face is new to me: I was supposed to have another one. But there is one thing that worries me: I am threatened by indifference, by what you might call a desert of the emotions. If I don't feel anything anymore, I will wither and die. None of us are ordinary people, not the Consul, not you or me. So we might as well laugh. And just get by. Let's not let time get bored while we're here. Let's make sure we give it some satisfaction, a little fantasy, for example, a little color. The Consul adores the subtleties of colors. Hardly surprising for a blind man."

My words seemed to soothe the Seated Woman. Her eyes were wet with tears as I spoke. She had lost her usual hard look. Her face showed no sign of the hatred on which she claimed to feed. I had managed to soften her, to move her. Yet I had not said anything particularly stirring. After a brief silence, she seized my hands and covered them with kisses. I was embarrassed. I tried to pull them away, but she held on tight. Her kisses were full of tears.

"I'm sorry," she said. "Forgive me for speaking to you so harshly. You are an angel, sent by the prophets. We are your slaves."

"That's enough!" I cried, to end that painful scene. "I am not an angel, and nobody sent me. Get up!"

We could hear the droning sound of the typewriter. It was as if the Consul was stubbornly tapping out the same word over and over.

A
CONFUSION
OF FEELINGS

I had trouble getting to sleep. I could hear the Seated Woman crying in a corner as the Consul paced up and down in his room. For a moment I thought to leave that house and try my luck elsewhere. But something held me back. Partly, of course, it was my interest in the Consul, and the turmoil my presence there was arousing in me. I also had a clear premonition that I would meet only strange people and have only unsettling relations wherever I went. I was firmly convinced that this family—this couple—was my destiny. They lay on my path. I had to enter that house, where my character would inevitably arouse turmoil. For the moment, there was a confusion of feelings. Nothing was clear. Who loved

99

whom? Who sought to perpetuate this situation? How could I leave that house without melodrama?

I found out that the Seated Woman had not allowed women in the house for a long time. She kept her brother jealously under her thumb. He would rebel, but he needed her. I think I arrived at that house when the tension was about to explode irreparably.

I who was emerging from a long absence, an illness, was becoming useful. Granted, the Seated Woman was unbalanced. She bore a hatred of humanity and reserved all the love in the world for her brother. Now and then she mentioned a truckdriver who used to meet her in strange places: the bakery next to the baths, or the potter's workshop on the edge of town. Once they met just before midnight in a mosque. Wrapped in gray jellabas, they passed unnoticed. They fell asleep in each other's arms and were awakened by the dawn prayers. They fled like thieves. The truckdriver never came back, and the Seated Woman had finally given up waiting for him. When she was delirious, she would tell this story over and over and claim that the Consul was the child of that idyll, that she told everyone that he was her brother because she could not admit that he was her illegitimate son. None of it was true. She was just raving.

The next day a new incident peaked the tension that kept us alive. The Consul came home late. He was tired; something had irritated him. The Seated Woman rushed to help him out of his jellaba. He reached out to push her away, but she ducked his hand and seconds later was holding the jellaba. She went to the kitchen to heat water to massage his feet. I stood motionless, watching the scene. He was furious.

"They're laughing at me! It's absolutely intolerable!"

He took off his dark glasses and wiped them nervously.

"The bitches! They stuck me with the one-eyed woman. The one nobody wants."

"That'll teach you to go without me," the Seated Woman called from the kitchen. "They never would have done that if I was there. Sit down, the water's hot."

The Consul sat in his armchair. She came in with the hot water, a towel over her shoulder. She knelt and took her brother's right foot. When his foot touched the water, the Consul cried out and knocked his sister over with a sudden movement. As she tumbled, her head nearly hit the corner of the table.

"The water's boiling hot," he said. "You did it on purpose, to punish me for going there. Go away! I don't want you here. The Guest will massage my feet from now on."

His tone changed as he asked if I would please do him that favor.

The Seated Woman glared at me. I felt sorry for her. She was unhappy—hurt and humiliated.

"Go ahead, you may as well," she said.

In fact I had no desire to massage that petty dictator's feet. But I couldn't refuse without triggering another outburst. I went over to him and said without raising my voice:

"Do it yourself for a change."

I left him there, his feet in the basin, and joined the Seated Woman in the kitchen. I understood why she was angry, but I wanted to know more.

"You want to know everything!"

"That's right," I said.

"It's all my fault. I have never refused him anything. I

101

satisfied his every whim. Since you've been here, he has wanted to do without me, wanted you to take my place. I'm not blaming you. But you should be aware that he's completely unpredictable. It's better not to love him, to keep a protective veil between him and everyone else."

She took a chair and began to talk, her voice hushed.

"At first it was once a month, then twice, then three times. He made me go with him. I would describe the women to him. It was embarrassing, of course. We would go in through a secret door. No one was supposed to see us. The madam was very understanding. She would sit us down in a room and have the girls file by. My job was to answer specific questions about each girl's skin color, eye color, chest and waist measurements, whether she had gold teeth—he hates gold teeth. I would do what he asked, then wait outside in the street. That was the worst part: waiting while the Consul did his business. It sometimes took quite a while. I would think about him, think about my life, a bitter taste in my mouth, as if my saliva held all the world's bitterness. 'As long as he is satisfied,' I would tell myself. Then remarkable peace and calm would settle over the house. He became placid, attentive, even affectionate. I would bless the woman who had soothed him. One day I thought of finding him a wife. He refused. I then realized that his pleasure was to go with me to that forbidden place. I realized that the blind need specific situations to fuel their imagination, because images do not exist for them, at least not the way as they do for us. In the end I took pleasure in going with him and helping him choose the woman. But since you've been here, he goes to the girls without telling me. I understand: he wants to be free himself, he doesn't want me to be the eye of his desire anymore. It couldn't last. In reality I was the eye of sin. And that kind of thing shouldn't exist between brother and sister. But there are so many things between us that shouldn't exist.

"When he was small, I used to wash him. I would soap him, rub him, rinse him, dry him. As if he was my doll. He obviously loved it, until the day that this pleasure—how shall I put it?—was preceded by desire. He put his head on my breast and clung to me. His face was flushed, his eyes wide open like those of a man lost and wandering in the desert. 'I want you to wash me,' he said. He was no longer a child. He stayed alone in the washroom for a long time. Then I went to clean the floor. I don't know whether he had urinated or done something else, but there was filth everywhere, a little like at the baths in late morning after the men have gone. He said nothing. I said nothing. I'd have done anything to make him happy. Even now I'd stoop to anything to keep him. Then you came along. You're our savior, an angel who knows everything. You will damn us or save us. The exterminating angel will clean up this spiderweb. Or perhaps become our accomplice.

"Now you know a lot. It will not be easy for you to extract yourself from this hell. Hell or paradise—that's for you to decide. We are people of the night: the Consul carries it in his eyes forever, while I seek it obsessively. And you, you must have been born on a night of uncertain moon, a night when the stars were within reach of all hopes, perhaps on that terrible night when fates are sealed, when every Muslim feels the shudder of death. When I saw you come into the baths, gripped by cold and panic, I could see in your eyes that you had been sent by the last Night of Destiny. I knew at once that you were alone in the world: without parents, family, or friends. You must be one of those exceptional creatures born of absolute solitude. I was waiting for you. On the twenty-seventh night of Ramadan I had a clear vision that stopped my heart. I too, though I am not a good Muslim, felt the slight shudder of death run through my body. I saw a silhouette lean over the Consul's bed and kiss him on the forehead. I thought it was death. I rushed into his room and found him crying like a child. He wept, but he did not know why. He spoke of our mother for the first time. He was convinced that she was alive and was going to visit us. I held him in my arms and rocked him like a baby; I gave him my breast. He fell back asleep with his lips still on my breast."

THE
CONSUL'S
ROOM

S o my destiny was sealed. I had become essential to that unusual couple.

The night before some holiday—I forget which one—the Consul brought two live chickens home. Taking advantage of his sister's absence, he decided to kill them himself. Anything that might call attention to the Consul's infirmity was scrupulously avoided, but when I saw him standing on the terrace with a chicken in one hand and a straight razor in the other, I was afraid. The blade gleamed in the sunlight. The Consul was excited at the thought of cutting the chickens' heads off. I offered to help. He said no. He crouched on the ground, stepping on the wings to hold the chicken down, grabbed the bird with his left hand, and slit its throat with his right. The chicken flapped around, spattering walls and clothes with blood. It lay twitching in a corner as the Consul, pleased with himself, began the same operation with the other chicken. He was sweating, almost jubilant. But this time he was careless and cut his left index finger. There was blood everywhere. The Consul wrapped his finger in a handkerchief. It must have hurt, but he didn't show it. He didn't laugh as much. It had been a half success. As I cleaned up the blood on the terrace, I smelled paradise incense, small pieces of black wood burned on holidays. The smell brought with it memories of a holiday with a lot of music. I must have been three or four. I was in my father's arms as he handed me, legs slightly apart, to a barber who did circumcisions. I saw the blood again, my father's sudden but deft gesture, his hand splattered with blood. There was blood on my thighs too, and on my white saroual.

It was a scented memory tinged with blood. I laughed to myself, then thought of the madness of my pigheaded father, trapped in the vortex of misfortune. I put my hand on my belly unconsciously, as if to reassure myself, then went back to washing the terrace.

The Consul bandaged his finger. He was proud of himself despite everything. I laughed at the ridiculous situation my father had put himself in. The Consul suffered in silence, believing that he had risen to the challenge of his blindness.

An atmosphere now of suspicion, now of complicity had settled over the house. I was drawn deeper and deeper into a drama that had long been underway. I was the missing character who arrived just as the conflicts had been winding down, the drama hovering on the brink of a burlesque tragedy mingling blood and laughter. I was even beginning to wonder whether the Seated Woman and the Consul—supposedly brother and sister, ghosts come out of some age-old night blackened by the vomiting of a ruined soul—were even related. Maybe it was all just a game in which life itself was a mere accoutrement, a piece of folklore. Perhaps the Seated Woman was a professional stage director, the Consul a pervert pretending to be blind, and I the prey in some imagined hunt along a clifftop. I told myself that I had lived too long in lies and pretense not to realize that this was a strange, even sordid affair. I decided to redouble my vigilance, to be ready for an honorable exit or a sudden flight.

I began to examine things as I tidied up the Consul's room, discreetly looking through the things in the cupboard, which I had never opened before. Clothes were carefully folded on one side; on the other were drawers filled with all kinds of things. In the top drawer were several bunches of keys, most of them rusty; old keys, broken keys, locks blackened by layers of dust, nails of every shape and size.

I gently shut that drawer and opened another at random. There I found something like twenty watches, all of them working but each showing a different time. Some were of gold, others of silver.

Another drawer held all kinds of glasses and monocles: sunglasses, prescription glasses, glasses with a lens missing or with both missing. In the back was a packet of papers tied with string. They were ophthalmologists' prescriptions, opticians' bills, advertising brochures for vision products. The dates were all very old.

I continued my search, trying to establish some link

between the contents of the various drawers. I opened another. It was lined with embroidered cloth. Several barbers' razors were laid out carefully, open, their blades gleaming. A sheep's eye in a bottle swam in a yellowish liquid. It looked at me. You would have thought it was alive and was watching over the razors. I felt sick and shut the drawer.

What I found next sent a shiver down my spine. The bottom drawer seemed to be empty, but as I was about to close it, I noticed that it was not as deep as the others. I pulled it all the way open, pushed a partition, and saw a well-polished revolver, in perfect working order. It was unloaded. Three magazines of bullets were piled beside it.

Why did he keep this weapon? I was intrigued, but not disturbed, by his collections. Yet that revolver—brand new—frightened me. Was it for murder or suicide? I sat on the edge of the bed and tried to puzzle out the meaning of all those accumulated objects. Across from me I saw the typewriter, a packet of white paper, a folder of typed pages. I got up and carefully opened the file. I leafed through it, reading at random. It was a journal, but also a story, with pasted bits of paper and chaotic drawings.

On one page this reflection was underlined in red: "How can one go beyond death? There are those who have erected statues for the purpose. Some are very beautiful. Others are awful. I know them better than those who look at them. I touch them. Caress them. Measure their thickness and immobility. That is not the answer. I shall leave behind neither a statue nor a street name, but a gesture, one that some will consider absurd, others sublime; good Muslims will think it heretical, while those who know death and who set cemeteries ablaze will find it heroic. This gesture will take death by surprise, will anticipate it, make it bend, and lay it in a pile of straw that will be set on fire by innocent hands, by the hands of children stilled by the unbearable light this gesture will leave."

I heard footsteps in the alleyway. It was the Consul coming home. I quickly put things in order and went back to the cleaning. The Consul arrived with a big bouquet of flowers and handed them to me.

"These are for you," he said. "I picked them out myself, one by one. We rarely give people flowers. But your patience and presence deserve them."

He sat in the armchair. As I was about to heat the water for his feet, he said:

"Where are you going? I don't want you to take care of me like a maid anymore. No more washbasins, no more foot massages. That's over with. You deserve much better. On the other hand, I am eager for you to be a partner in my thoughts. I like having you near me when I read or write. I have to confess that I started writing again when you came into this house. You know that I am not a simple man. I try to make blindness an advantage and refuse to consider it an infirmity. That sometimes makes me unfair. I do things that involve taking risks. You must have wondered what it is I'm writing. One of these days I'll have you read certain pages. My world is largely inside me. I furnish it with my own creations: I am forced to resort to what inhabits my dark room. You would be astonished, even embarrassed, if I told you all it contains. It is my secret. No one has access to it, not even my sister.

"I am surrounded by objects. There are some I can

master, but others are indomitable. Try to master a razor, for instance, or a pair of scissors that cut everything in their path. So I'm suspicious. I must admit I'm terrified of anything with a cutting edge. Maybe that's why I insisted on slaughtering the chickens myself the other day. I cut myself, but it isn't serious. Imagine if the razor had slipped from my hand: surely it would have cut off my nose or all five fingers. I'm not trying to scare you. I envy you. I wish I was in your place. You are an observer, a witness, sometimes an actor. You are lucky to have been invited to share in the life of a house without having to know or accept the past that has shaped us. That is why I have made no attempt to pry into your past either. I rely only on my intuition and my emotions. Now put those flowers in a vase."

I thanked him and left him rubbing his forehead, trying to banish a headache. He became fragile and disoriented when his head hurt. It made him aware of his infirmity. He cried for help as I was looking around for somewhere to put the vase. I rushed in and found him waving his arms, in a panic because he could not find his painkillers, which were right behind him, well within reach.

"I can't breathe with this pain," he said. "It's like a hammer smashing a block of marble. Every blow is a jolt."

I gave him the pills with a glass of water and put my cold hand on his forehead. At first, he could not bear my touch, but he felt better when I massaged him.

"Go on," he said, "this is good for me. Your hands are full of kindness. I was born with migraine, and it has pursued me all my life. That is my main infirmity."

I made him coffee and helped him to bed, not to sleep but to rest from the effects of the attack. He took my hand

and would not let me leave. I found it quite natural to rest my hand in his. I felt his warm body. We spent much of the afternoon like that. When I heard the key in the lock, I got up and went to open the door. I had closed the safety catch. The Seated Woman looked surprised. She asked me why I had locked myself in. "It was an accident," I said. She let it drop. I told her about her brother's migraine. She was upset. I stopped her from going to wake him up. Later in the evening, she asked me:

"Do you remember that time the Consul came home furious? It must have been at least a month ago."

"Maybe more. But what does that have to do with today's attack?"

"Yes, of course, you have no way of knowing. But I see a connection between abstinence and headaches. When a man keeps that cloudy water inside him too long, it rises to the head and causes pain, because it's not the head that needs it. Do you understand?"

"Vaguely. Do you mean that a man who doesn't let his semen out regularly gets headaches? What about women?"

"They get irritable. They shout about nothing. But I'm used to it. I don't even shout anymore."

I laughed softly to myself. The Seated Woman gave a little smile, then burst out in loud laughter. She put a hand over her mouth and tried to stop.

A
LAKE
OF
HEAVY
WATER

I spent the night fighting currents of heavy, sticky water in a deep lake peopled by all kinds of plants and animals. A stifling smell, thick and undefinable, rose from those waters, dead but roiled from within by the scurryings of rats playing with an injured cat.

I could see everything in the stagnant yet somehow moving water. I was in a glass cage, and a hand pushed me to the bottom and brought me up again at will. I felt smothered, but my shouts could not escape the cage. I recognized the body of Fatima, my poor epileptic cousin to whom I had been married to keep up appearances and whom I loved because she was a gaping wound deprived of all affection. Her face was serene, her body intact. She lay at the bottom of the lake like some old object nobody wanted. Oddly, the rats left her alone. When I saw her I shouted so loudly that I woke up terrified, dripping with sweat.

It was not the first time I had had that kind of nightmare. In each one I saw a face from my past. To forget completely was impossible. What could I do to stop feeling guilty, to stop being hounded by rats and spiders?

I thought of the theory of cloudy water rising to the head and began to laugh. I would have to pay tribute one way or another, here or elsewhere. That much was clear. If it would speed the process of forgetting, I would not quarrel with destiny's rules and regulations.

So it was that I emerged from a heavy nightmare as the Consul cast off the pain racking his head. We were both emerging from the same ordeal, which reminded us that we were both cursed. That freed us. We felt freer just because we knew that the ghosts of our past would catch up to us in the end.

That morning, my body still weary, I decided to take another step closer to the Consul. As he was leaving the house for school, I asked him not to be late coming home. He looked surprised.

"You sound like my sister. I'll be home early, just to make you happy. I won't go to the café, and I won't stop to see my friend the barber."

I wanted to go with him to the women. The Seated Woman would never find out. He would show me the way. I liked this preposterous idea, whose audacity appealed to me. I was curious. My body felt lighter, forever relieved of the weight of the night's dead water. The feeling of cheer gave me gooseflesh. I leaped about like a madwoman as I did the housework. I spent a long time in the bathroom, washing and scenting myself as if I were going to a wedding.

The Consul came home about five. He brought a sheaf of mint and some pastries. I told him that both would have to wait and that the Seated Woman had told me to take him to the women. He stood stock-still in surprise, then swallowed. He drank a glass of water, then he asked me if his sister had really assigned me such a mission. He was incredulous.

"This is very embarrassing. It's between my sister and me. It's not possible."

As he spoke, I saw that his face lit up at the idea of going to the women.

"Would you really take me there? You wouldn't be embarrassed?"

"Not at all. I'm curious. It would be a chance to go someplace I'd never see. With you I have an excuse."

"Well, if that's how you see it, what can I do but follow?"

After a short pause, he added:

"Or rather, you will follow me."

"I'll take your arm, and you tell me where to turn."

It was the first time I had walked in the street holding a man's arm. We looked like a normal couple. Nothing at all unusual about us. If some ill-intentioned eye had followed us and found out where we were going, perhaps it would have put an evil spell on us and cursed us to the end of time. That eye was there, behind a door left ajar.

A woman watched unseen. As I passed close by her, I felt struck by an arrow and shuddered. A wave of misfortune had been set in motion. My body sensed it like a sign, an apprehension. I preferred to make light of it and continued on my way. We passed the celebrated building, easily recognizable. The Consul told me not to stop. I followed him. He led me into a dark alleyway and we went in through a low door in an unlit corridor. For once we were even, surrounded by the same darkness.

"Don't be afraid. There's a step."

I held his arm so tight it hurt him. We went up the stairs and came to a closed door. The Consul knocked twice, then a third time. A woman, the madam, let us in and greeted the Consul:

"Long time no see. You have a new companion?"

"Make us some tea, please, not too sweet."

She took us into a sordid room with a none-too-clean sink. The faucet dripped. In the back was an old cupboard smelling of mothballs. I sat in a chair. The Consul stretched out comfortably on the bed. He took out a pipe already filled with kif and lit it. He smoked alone. We waited in silence for the tea. I looked around, my eyes wide, taking in everything. I was impatient. A little girl, barely ten years old, brought us a tray with a teapot and glasses, then disappeared without a word. We were drinking the tea—too sweet—when the madam came in, followed by two women in their early twenties. They were neither ugly nor beautiful, but clearly had no desire to stay with the Consul. The Consul asked me to describe them.

"One is dark, and has tattoos on her forehead and chin. Her hair is oiled and gathered in a brightly colored scarf. She has big but sagging breasts. She has a belly. Her butt is fat, her legs are hairy, and she's chewing gum. She's looking at you, and making a face. She's not beautiful,

116

not ugly either. Takes no pleasure in her work. The other one is thin. She has beautiful breasts and a trim waist, but a huge butt. Her hair is black, her eyes light. She isn't chewing gum, but she has a twitch; she spits all the time. It's up to you."

The madam, who had gone out, came back.

"Which one is staying?" she asked.

"Neither one," the Consul answered from his bed.

When the three of them had left the room, the Consul handed me some money.

"I forgot to give you the money to pay."

It was a not inconsiderable sum. We waited for a while and a beautiful young woman came in, frightened, as though the madam had pushed her in from the other side of the door. She looked at us, bewildered, not knowing what this man and this woman wanted from her. I noticed she was trembling; she must have been new to the business. The madam reappeared, apparently pleased with her choice. She held out her hand and I gave her the money. She was about to leave when I began my description of the young woman, who was almost blonde and had large, firm breasts:

"She is very thin, dark, with little breasts, a narrow waist, short hair, a well-balanced butt, plump lips. She isn't chewing gum. She wants you."

I motioned to the madam and the young woman. They left, and I waited for the Consul's answer.

"You say she has small breasts and a well-balanced butt? All right, I'll take her."

I had already taken off my jellaba and my dress. I went quietly to the bed and undid the Consul's saroual. I left the dim room light on, climbed up, and straddled him.

117

Slowly I let him penetrate me, holding his shoulders to stop him from changing position. He came very quickly. I stayed on top of him, motionless, waiting for him to recover his energy. Not long afterwards, he had an enormous erection again. Complete lack of modesty or embarrassment made up for my inexperience. Desire directed my body by instinct, dictating the appropriate movements. I had gone mad. In a brothel with a blind man I was discovering pleasure for the first time in my life! He was insatiable. Neither of us said a word. I stifled my moans. I could not let him realize the deception. When he finally dozed off, I dressed quickly and knocked at the door.

"Don't come in yet. I'm dressing."

He got up, taking his time. I crouched in a corner. I knew he had not been fooled, but I wanted the afternoon's events to be shrouded in doubt. Our bodies were bound in a complicity of silence and secrecy. Most of all we could not speak, could not put into words an apparent lie that was in fact a truth that could not be spoken.

When I closed my eyes that night, I found myself back in the lake of heavy water. But the cage was gone. I dived in and easily swam back to the surface by myself. The land around looked much as it had the night before. There was an abandoned park, with red grass and bare trees. A swing—broken and untouched, like an old piece of junk—hung from a branch of an enormous fig tree. Unconsciously, I touched my forehead, looking for a scar. It was hidden under my hair. I used to go to that park with my father. Dressed as a boy, I would tease the little girls, until one day the brother of one of them knocked me out of the swing. My face was covered with blood, and I cried. The brother, who was older than me, said before running off, "If you were a girl, I'd have done something else to you." My father, panic-stricken, rushed me to the hospital. I had completely forgotten the incident.

My dream ended with a violent gust of wind that lifted the dead leaves weighed down by lichen and carried off the unused swing, whose desolate presence recalled distant memories.

In the morning I did not have the heart to face the Consul. I had retained his scent and sweat. But he knocked at my door, bringing me a glass of orange juice he had prepared himself, testimony to his tender affection. I blushed, a warm flush rising within me that made me clumsy. He sat on the edge of the bed, took out an embroidered handkerchief, and held it out to me. Our fingers touched. I thanked him. He said nothing. I felt, deep down, as an evident, natural truth, that this man had a remarkable quality, a kind of grace that had been suppressed by the Seated Woman's brutal possession of him, which he accepted so as to avoid tragedy.

He had no need to talk. His gaze, which rested nowhere, disturbed me. There was sometimes an uneasy gentleness about him, probably the product of pure animality. A silent intimacy had filled that room so used to solitude. We could hear people passing in the street outside, yet we dared not speak. I slowly moved my hand close to his, then pulled it back. I was afraid of breaking something fragile, something that I could neither name nor forget. I felt as if we had been deliberately sealed up in a tomb, as if we ourselves were a secret to be closely guarded. There are intense moments when just one presence is enough, and something powerful, perhaps even decisive, occurs. You cannot say what it is, but for some obscure reason emotion alone reveals it, and you are ignited by it, as happy as a child transported by joy to a world of wonders. I had never dreamed that one day I would reach that state in which body and feelings seemed to float, bearing me to summits of pure air. A high mountain wind blew through my thoughts. Confusion had vanished. I was at peace with myself.

The Consul got up. I wanted to stop him, to keep him near me, to touch him, to run my lips over his neck, to remain in his arms. But I didn't move, for fear of ruining everything. He left the room without a word. My mind had been blank during those moments of silence in his presence. I did not want to think about the Seated Woman's reaction or about the new atmosphere that would now prevail in the house. It was too soon.

The Seated Woman was still asleep. The Consul had gone out. I didn't know what to do that morning. I decided to stay in my room.

THE
BROTHEL
CHARADE

W|e played out the brothel charade for some time, out of desire for silence and secrecy more than out of fear of arousing the Seated Woman's suspicions. Her role and status in the house had shrunk in just a few days. Though she did not react, I did not think she would allow herself to be ousted from the stage entirely. She had a lot of work to do at the time. Apart from the baths, she was arranging marriages.

One evening she came home late and spoke to me as though I had asked her for a favor or for some piece of information:

"That's it, I've got what you need."

"What do you mean?"

"Don't play dumb with me. You know what it is. It's

what you think about all the time, what keeps you up at night."

"A lot of things keep me up at night."

"Yes, but this is like an itch, like a worm under the skin that you can't pin down and scratch once and for all."

Of course I knew very well what she was talking about, but I was trying to provoke her vulgarity, which would make her lose her temper. Especially since the Consul would never have suspected that his sister had become a rather dubious marriage-broker.

"All right," she said, "let's not beat around the bush. I've found a man for you. A widower, but still in good shape. Impressive resources. He was looking for an orphan girl, an unattached woman, someone alone in the world. You fit the bill, don't you?"

The Consul listened to this exchange without comment.

"I don't want to get married. I never asked you for any such thing."

"That's true, you didn't. But in this house I'm the one who decides who gets married and who stays single."

She had raised her voice, suddenly becoming authoritarian and inflexible. Her brother frowned. She grabbed me, dragged me to the kitchen and locked me in. She was absolutely furious and was now trying to turn the Consul against me. I was afraid, because she seemed to know things about my past. Someone must have talked to her. She lowered her voice when she spoke to her brother, but I put my ear against the door and heard some of it.

"She's a usurper and a liar. She's dangerous. She lied to us, and I have proof. She is stronger than you think.

That woman has led a life of betrayal. It seems that she killed her parents. Her mother died mad and her father was never even sick before he died. We're sheltering a thief and a murderess in this house. Did you know she ran off with the family inheritance? You must believe me, my brother, my life, light of my eyes."

"Enough! I don't believe you. You're jealous, and crazy too. You made this story up to cast me back into loneliness and servitude. It won't work."

Rejected by the Consul, who locked himself in his room, she screamed at the top of her lungs:

"That woman is a man! I have proof, photographs, papers. She's tricked us."

The Consul burst out laughing. The Seated Woman went on shouting, then I heard her begging:

"No, brother, no. Come on, you're frightening me. Put the razor down, you'll hurt yourself. Please! All right, it's not true, I made the whole thing up. You know how much I love you and how unhappy I am. I take it all back."

"Then open the kitchen door."

She did.

The Consul was standing there furious and determined, a straight razor at his throat. I took his hand and led him to his room. He was trembling and drenched with sweat. I took the razor away and sat down beside him.

"My eyes are dry," he said, "but I am weeping inside. I weep because my sister is mad, and because I might lose you. I won't be able to stand it if you leave. I don't even know your name. From the very first day I've called you 'the Guest.' I could have given you a name, but names and family ties don't matter. You have brought a bit of life and feeling, warmth and grace, to this madhouse."

The Seated Woman had gone out again. I took the opportunity of this crisis to confess everything to the Consul. I told him the whole story, from my birth to my flight, including my wanderings, the rape, my encounter with the Seated Woman. I told him of my regrets, my sadness, and the hope I had rediscovered thanks to his quiet, tender friendship. I told him that I knew they would find me and punish me someday, that I was waiting with resignation for that day, but that I too could not bear being separated from him.

He smiled at my story. He considered it a tale I had concocted to account for the first twenty years of my life, the imaginary story of a bored child who dealt with serious matters through laughter.

"Laughter is important," he said. "It breaks the wall of fear, intolerance, and fanaticism."

We were still recovering from the Seated Woman's outburst. He was very good at talking his way through an unpleasant situation.

"I don't have to close my eyes," he said. "I can sit right here and my mind drifts to the other room or out onto the terrace. I like to laugh when nothing goes right, because nothing is ever completely clear or completely obscure. The way I see it, everything is complex, and the truth is closer to the shadow than to the tree that casts the shadow. If what you have told me really happened, then you must have had a lot of fun. But I wouldn't say the same for your parents and the people around you. You were lucky to be able to play two roles so subtly. As I told you once, blindness is not an infirmity. Or at least not for someone who knows how to use it. Using it does not mean deceit; it means revealing the virtues of the obscure. It's like intelligence, which someone once defined as the failure to comprehend the world. Which recalls our mystical poets, for whom appearance was the most perverse mask of truth. You know from your own experience that clarity is a delusion. How can anything be clear and definable in the relations between two people? It sounds to me as though there was a moment of inattention in your life, a moment that lasted until you came to like it, took pleasure in it, and decided to use it to cover your tracks and to escape prying eyes."

He paused for a moment and felt for my hand. I made no effort to move closer to him. I was still thinking about what he had just said. "A moment of inattention." That was my life all right, or my semblance of one. I was convinced that had I met this man when I was disguised as a boy, I would have either loved or hated him, for he would have unmasked me at once. I was careful of appearances, but underneath I was the same, and this man without sight saw with all his other senses. It would have been impossible to lie to him. You can't lie to a blind man. You can tell him stories, but he trusts the voice more than the words spoken.

Though he pretended not to believe my story, his smile told me that he had suspected something. He took my hand, brought it to his lips, and kissed it, nibbling at it slightly. I gave a little cry.

"Our sin," he said with a dreamy air, "the thing that saps and spoils the soul, that gradually robs it of its purity, is our rejection of loneliness. But what can we do? We are all so vulnerable. Perhaps you and I, with our unique destinies, have learned to go beyond that fragility. That is what I felt the moment you came into this house. We owe nothing to anyone—that is our strength. We could leave this world at a moment's notice, with no fuss and no regrets. I have spent my whole life thinking about just such a voluntary departure. I carry my own death with me; I wear it on my sleeve. All the rest is just aimless thrashing to avoid disappointing time. We must not let time get bored with us. That would be stupid, unworthy of our intelligence. I say 'our' because we are alike, joined by a pact sealed in secrecy."

I thought about the Consul threatening to cut his throat if the Seated Woman did not let me out of the kitchen. I couldn't resist asking whether he had been serious. He claimed not to know and remarked that in any case seriousness is just a sharpened form of play. He may have been sincere. He admitted that he was sometimes afraid of his sister, and he described her in the most unflattering terms:

"She's a little crazy, because she's unhappy. She was very brave when we found ourselves destitute overnight, with no family, no home, no shelter. We were in ruins. The town had quaked, had slid toward a red horizon. Ever since then my sister has carried an inner fury that nothing has soothed or extinguished. She has grown bitter. She can be mean and unfair, and is capable of destroying everything, for no apparent reason. The only thing that makes her back off is an even greater violence. Which is why I sometimes get violent. Not against her, but against myself. That touches her inmost being. And she knows that I am capable of acting on my threats. What I blame her for most of all is her lack of generosity, her rather too obvious inclination to hatred and nastiness. I am her prisoner, I know that. It grieves me, and I hope to break free someday. Just think of it! I have been able to free myself of the shackles of blindness, but not of the affection my sister lavishes upon me."

I had moved closer to him as he spoke and was now in his arms, feeling his warm body.

We made love in the house for the first time. Then we lay in silence. I thought of the Seated Woman's threats and schemes again. She was quite capable of destroying us, or me at least. There had been spittle in the corner of her mouth as she screamed that morning. An outward sign of hatred. Her eyes were not red anymore, but yellow. She was like a furious wounded animal that refuses to die alone. She must have found out some bits of information about my past. Though I had nothing to apologize for about that part of my life, I wanted to avoid being confronted with the masquerade. When I buried my father, I had been careful to inter all the objects I had used during that time. There was no evidence. The uncles, sisters, cousins, and neighbors were still around, of course. But I had wiped out all traces and fled to the other end of the country. My wanderings, as it happened, did not last long. Fate led me to the baths. It was the rape in the forest that drove me there. I knew that for a while I would be able to live only with strange people. I was pleased that the first man to love my body was blind, a man with eyes in his fingertips and whose soft and slow caresses had reshaped my image. That was my victory; I owed it to the Consul, whose grace was expressed through touch. He had restored vitality to each of my

127

slumbering, fettered senses. When we made love he spent long moments staring at my body with his hands. He had not only awakened my desire, but also gave a rare intensity that he satisfied magnificently, in silence and soft light. He was very concerned about the light. Sometimes he would be clumsy and get irritated. Then he would ask me to light another lamp or candle. "I need a little light to see your body," he would say, "to breathe its scent, to let my lips trace the lines of its harmony." His experience with women was probably limited; he would concentrate like an artist about to begin a new work. He compared himself to a sculptor. "I have to sculpt patiently and carefully," he would say, "so that your body becomes familiar to me and ceases to rebel."

I had spent my adolescence rejecting desire with all my strength, until finally I no longer even thought about it. I had no right to it. I got by with my delirious dreams peopled by phalluses, ephebi, and vulgar orgies. Often I would ease my body myself, and then feel ashamed. All that seemed very remote now. I did not want to think about it anymore. The miracle had the Consul's face and eyes. He had carved me into a statue of flesh, eager and desired. I was no longer a creature of sand and dust, of uncertain identity, crumbling at the slightest gust of wind. I felt each of my limbs growing firm, solidifying. No longer was I a creature whose skin was but a mask, an illusion designed to deceive a shameless society based on hypocrisy and the myths of a twisted religion, an illusion devoid of spirit, a delusion fabricated by a father obsessed with shame. To be reborn and to live I needed to forget, to roam, to find grace distilled by love. But the happiness, the fulfillment, the self-discovery I had found in a blind man's sublime gaze were not to last. I knew that, felt it. My brief but intense happiness would be violently interrupted.

THE
MURDER

I   t all happened very fast. The Seated Woman had been gone for more than a week. The Consul thought she was busy with her marriages. I was convinced that she had gone on a journey in search of something. Before leaving she had sent a servant woman from the baths to tell us that she had a lot to do and that we should not worry.

She came back early one morning. I was fast asleep in the Consul's arms. She opened the door and dragged me out of bed by the hair. The Consul woke up with a terrified jolt, thinking he was having a nightmare. She was screaming, foaming at the mouth:

"Come here, you bitch! Thief! Whore, come and look

who's waiting for you downstairs! You killed them both and ran off with the inheritance."

She pushed and kicked me. I grabbed at anything I could reach. The Consul got dressed as she pushed me down the stairs. I fell, and when I picked myself up at the bottom, I found myself staring at my uncle, Fatima's father, the miser my father had told me to be careful of. He was cold with rage, his face drained by a pallor that boded ill. I knew he was a cruel man, and that his wickedness had made his daughter a neglected epileptic. My father used to call him "my brother rancor." He was the one who taunted my mother—coldly and cynically—for not giving birth to a boy. The snot that hung from his nose was poison. I had always hated him, but I was stronger because I never let him get close to me or have the slightest contact with me. I knew he harbored boundless hatred. I went along with the fake marriage to Fatima mainly to get her away from her family, who left her all alone during her seizures. My uncle had spent his whole life envying his brother and trying to hurt people. He loved to set traps, to trick people, and to take advantage of their weakness or misfortune. He was a son of a bitch. The moment I laid eyes on him, I knew he had trapped me. He stood in silence, savoring his victory. I could have denied everything and pretended not to recognize him, but the image of the lake with the heavy, sticky water swept over me, and I got nauseous and lost my self-control. We stared at each other. In his eyes I saw hatred and lust for revenge. In mine there was pity and an immense desire to get it over with. I asked him to wait while I got my things. I went up to the Consul's room: he looked shattered, helpless, and numb. I went straight to the bottom drawer, loaded the pistol, and went slowly down-stairs. When I was a yard away from my uncle, I emptied the pistol into his body.

In a split second I knew that this was the end of the episode. It was my duty to finish it, to put my signature on it with that murder. I sank into a morass of thoughts and images. I was swept up in their flow and knew that my hand had been moved by Fatima's energy, by my father's and mother's, and by everyone who had ever fallen victim of that man's wickedness.

I was relieved when I saw the greenish-yellow blood flowing from the body as it lay on the ground. The Seated Woman howled and clawed her cheeks. The Consul, pris-oner of his own silence, seemed distracted. I was cold. I wrapped a scarf around my shoulders and waited for things to take their course. I stared at the ground, no longer hearing anything. I was already far away, running through a meadow pursued by a pack of children throw-ing stones at me. I was at a happy age now, barely a year old. I no longer had any notion of loss. I had lived with such passion for these few months that it could nourish me to the end of my days.

I was tried and sentenced to fifteen years in prison. I did not want a lawyer. The court appointed one for me, a young woman who delivered a superb summation about the condition of women in Muslim countries. The Seated Woman and the Consul appeared as witnesses. I can't remember what she said. As for the Consul, if it was an ordeal for him, he did not show it. He made a prepared statement to the court:

"He who seeks to shame a man is unworthy of our esteem. He who spares no one shame is not a man. One who has grace and whose soul is endowed with greatness may sometimes become cruel, and may thus dispense justice. The woman on trial here today is one of those exceptional beings who survive all the shame hatred can inflict. She went out to meet her greatest pain, an act dictated by the greatness of her soul. I am bound to that woman by a pact, by our own secret. That is our love. It is unusual to hear talk of love in this place. But be advised that the love that binds us lifts the darkness from me. I will wait for her."

IN
THE
DARKNESS

M y life in prison soon fell into a routine. I did not consider imprisonment a punishment. Finding myself behind bars made me realize how much my life as a man had been like a prison. I had been confined to a single role, and in that sense deprived of freedom. Beyond the limits of that role lay catastrophe. At the time I had not been aware of how much I had suffered. My destiny had been twisted, my instincts suppressed, my body transfigured, my sexuality denied, my hopes destroyed. And I had had no choice.

Prison is a place where life is simulated. It has the color of absence, of a long day without light. It is a sheet, a narrow shroud, a parched face abandoned by life.

My cell was small and I was glad of it. It seemed to

foreshadow my grave; my stay there was like preparation for the great leavetaking. I was not bothered by the dampness of the walls. I was content to have a territory proportionate to my body. I had as little as possible to do with the other prisoners. I refused to go out for exercise walks. I asked for paper and a pencil. I wanted to write. Words seemed to beckon me from all sides, coming to me in packs, in large numbers, knocking at the wall of my cold cage. Words, smells, images, and sounds lurked around my captivity. At first I took no notice of them; I was learning how to wait. I did not want to measure time, so I blocked out the faint light that came in through an opening at the top of one wall. What was the point of simulating the brightness of day when everything was plunged into black night, long and deep? I wanted darkness, and in the end I got it. I preferred to live in a stretch of unvarying color, to get used to the flat terrain on which I walked. Little by little I entered the universe of those deprived of sight as I was deprived of freedom. I lived with my eyes shut. I blindfolded myself. Not only was there nothing to see in that sordid place, but it was my way of being close to the Consul. I tried to enter his darkness, hoping to meet him, touch him, and speak to him.

He came to visit every Friday, in the early afternoon. My life was punctuated by those weekly visits. At first this amused a few idiots who made sarcastic cracks about "the blind man who comes to see her—get it?—to see her." I never answered them. In the early days, before I closed my eyes, we would look at each other without speaking, holding hands for the whole visit. He brought me books, paper, pens. When I blindfolded myself, I had to give up writing. At the same time, my desire to write became ever more urgent. The lights were on in the cells from seven to nine at night. I decided to open my eyes and write during those two hours. I scribbled and scrawled. I had so many things to put down, but couldn't decide where to start. Then I would put the blindfold back on and bury my head in the pillow. It was reassuring to return to the darkness, where I was in communion with the Consul. He did not know what I was doing, and I didn't want him to know. My love for him was taking its own shortcuts, and that was the only way I could be with him.

Since I was unable to write properly, I used the two hours of light to read. I could not help interfering with all the characters in the stories I read. I would blindfold them and send them to prison for premeditated murder. My reading was never innocent. Sometimes I even trans-fered a character from one story to another. That was fun, and it gave me some scope for action. It all got mixed up in my head and came out at night, as dreams and night-mares to mingle and harass me. Little by little I myself became a character in those restless, fantastic nights, and I could not wait to get to sleep, where I had those un-common adventures.

I was caught up in a cruel love story in which I was both Sasuke, the disciple in love with his teacher, a music master, and Shunkin, the woman blinded by a kettle of boiling water poured on her face. I was both the man and the woman, now an angel possessed of grace and love, now a vengeful, pitiless storm. I was both musical note and instrument, passion and suffering. I lived through so many stories that I happily mixed them all together, curious to see how I would be garbed by each new night.

I read the *Thousand and One Nights*, of course, bit by bit. I leaped from night to night, well imagining the consequences of the disorder I was causing.

My nights were rich. I fed them with reading. I had annulled the days, immersing them in darkness, tying them all in the same sack. I had decided not to see anything of the prison, or at least as little as possible. That was my right and I insisted on it, despite occasional comments from the guards. The first year went by in that regular rhythm: darkness during the day, eyes open for reading or writing between seven and nine, darkness again with the night and its processions, the Consul's visit on Friday. It all became a ritual.

One Friday morning, I had a foreboding that he would not come. My heart was heavy, my mood bad. I couldn't say why, but I knew something was wrong.

At five o'clock the guard brought me a letter. The envelope had been opened. I took off my blindfold. It was too dark to make out the letter, so I climbed up on the bed and took down the piece of black cloth I had hung over the window. This gave me a trickle of light, and I began to read. My legs trembled and it was hard to open my eyes all the way. I waited for a moment.

Friend,

My sister died of a cerebral hemorrhage on Wednesday morning. I buried her all by myself that same day. She went quickly, thank goodness. Life in the house was unbearable. We were arguing constantly. I couldn't stand anything about her anymore: her habits, her food, her snoring, her smell, her voice. It was as though I was allergic to her very presence. I lost patience and snapped at her. I realize now how someone who is constantly and systematically frustrated can turn violent. My violence was physical at first; later, when things kept happening again, it became internal: I cultivated my hatred for that poor woman. Her whole life was a series of failed and unacknowledged ambitions and yearnings; she was determined to isolate me, to keep me for herself alone. She wanted to devour me. But I kept my head. I was watchful. After the tragedy and your departure, she said she felt guilty, but when she spoke of you, she said, "In any case, you could not expect anything true from someone whose life was built on lies." I let her talk. I never answered. She wept and hoped for death. Silently, I wished it on her. Her jealousy ruined us; she destroyed everything; nothing remains alive in our house.

She was the one who went to ask about you in your home village. She said she wanted to expose you. She managed to find that miserable uncle of yours, that usurer who used his shoe shop as a lending counter. Did you know that his death made many people happy? People had only contempt for him. He was involved in many suspicious dealings, but none of any real consequence. I'm telling you all this so you'll see that what you did was right.

I think about you. My eyes, closed on thoughts of you, wish to find you again. I have to settle the problems caused by my sister's death. I am not afraid of solitude. I don't know how long it will take to work everything out. I need someone to take care of the house and to light the stove in the kitchen for me. A young man, the son of some neighbors, is keeping me company for the moment. He reads to me and calls himself my disciple. I find that funny. His parents send me three meals a day. They are very kind. Their children go to my school. The day before yesterday I stopped receiving people; they come to offer help more than condolences. My sister was not well-liked. I think that must be the worst of it. To die alone and not be missed by anyone is so unbearably sad. I have always known that the iniquitous end their days in horrible loneliness. My sister did not have the time to experience that suffering, but she was unloved, and that made her suffer constantly. I was all she had in the world. Sometimes I did love her, and yielded to her requests. She insisted on taking care of everything, even washing me. I never loved her as a sister, but as a beggar who gives all she has in exchange for a little warmth. That is what pity is. I am being harsh, for I owe my survival to her. But must we carry with us all our lives those who condemn us to live? Now that she sleeps a soundless slumber free of images, a slumber beyond all nights, let us not awaken her with merciless judgment.

The suffering that dwells within me speaks not of her, but of you, day and night. My thoughts are rooted in the twilight forest where you are now held captive. My heart is a stone bench covered with leaves, placed on the roadside to offer rest to the weary. Chance or the wind will bring you back. I await you. Till we meet again.

I was moved by the death of the Seated Woman. I thought about her unhappiness, her barren body, her failures and the marks they had left on her face. I tried to understand why she could not resist doing evil. She wanted everyone else to pay for the wretchedness of her body, soon confused with the anguish of her soul. Some people draw their energy from hatred. You often see them at dusk, roaming around a lake of dead water, rats going before them to spill all their venom. However much they claim to be purifying themselves by secreting misfortune, the truth is that they bear negative charges which they must pass on to others before they cause their own paralysis and death. The Seated Woman had to die, a victim of her own determination to hurt others. Disturbed by the tragedy she herself had caused, she must have lost her mind, finding nowhere to discharge all her rancor.

I put my blindfold back on and sought the night again. There was nothing for me to do but wait out the placid hours that love alone would trouble. With all my being I sought calm, that state of slowed rhythms that brings relief and happy lassitude. All I wanted now was to sleep, to meet those characters who still lived within me, as if I were their storehouse, the hearth and crypt in which they lurked during daylight hours. But the moment I closed my eyes they rushed out from all over, chiding me for my long absence. I laughed, and with them I continued adventures begun in days gone by. What bothered me was that there was no trace of the Consul in that world so full of excitement, laughter, and fury. I had to find the secret door through which to bring him into those spectacles. True, there was a blind man, watchman at the gates of the Andalusian garden, but it was not the Consul. This man had a stick and stopped children from going in. Sometimes he even hit them. He was nasty, not because he could not see, but because he was a watchman and was poor.

THE
LETTER

W
ith the black blindfold I entered the world of the blind, little by little. I relearned the motions of daily life, reduced to a minimum in prison. I took off the blindfold only to read, write, and wash. The layer of darkness I drew over me thickened day by day. It helped me to separate from my body, the final caresses of the man I loved a burning memory now. Time was abolished of its own accord. Now I feigned nothing. I adapted, learning to tame loneliness and waiting. I was perhaps the only prisoner who never complained of loneliness. I imposed silence, even oblivion, around my cell. I paid to be left in peace. Most of all I did not want to have to justify my acts, or my inner isolation. A curious thing happened when I was imprisoned: I ceased to be

obsessed with my past as a woman disguised as a man.
I forgot all about it. With my uncle's death I had liquidated
the past (or so I thought). Besides, as I saw it, I was not
in prison to pay for that crime; I was there almost vol-
untarily, to await the Consul's return from some distant
continent. While I waited, I was learning to live in darkness. That seemed necessary to me if I were to deserve
his love. I adapted to my new life, cultivating patience.

The Consul's visits were more and more infrequent. He
preferred to write to me, and almost every letter repeated
that he suffered to see me in this state of reclusion and
submission. I clarified this misunderstanding in a letter
that took me a long time to write and an even longer time
to decide to send. I could not get used to the idea that
he would not read this letter directly but would hear it
from a third person. I had hoped to read it to him myself
in the visiting room, but they listened to our every word
there. I wished I knew how to write in braille. Today I
would have used one of those small tape recorders, but
this was before the days of cassettes. It was my first love
letter, and I must have rewritten it several times.

Friend,

*I leave it to humble words to tell you of the wavering
shadow of memory, which is all that remains of our poem. It
has now been several months, perhaps a century, that I have
been walking toward you, arms outstretched like the legen-
dary statue that goes to the sea. I am not following you, but
have instead taken the opposite path to meet you, that our
faces might be lit by the same light. I walk forward, and be-
neath my feet I feel a part of me taking root in the earth.
The thick layer of shadow I am building around me is my
sanctuary. It covers and protects me, now a mane, now a*

veil drawn against the light. You and I are of the same dream, just as others are of the same country. Like an echo of a morning song, your voice leans over me and comes with me as I walk. A bare voice, without words or sentences, just a murmur's warmth. The seasons pass here without touching us; they come and go behind the mountains. I say no prayer for our friendship, which you call love. It is beyond words. It is a plant with broad leaves anchored in my mind and in my heart. It prevents me from falling apart and from failing to wait. Sometimes sadness comes over me; a stupid, heavy sadness shrouds me like a cloak of dead stars. Then I do nothing. I let these moments that separate me from you pass. You draw away, your gaze averted. I know it, but can do nothing. I am nourished by the emotion I feel at the mere thought of you. I walk in time that is a desert, the sand sometimes cold, sometimes searing. I wear thick, woolen socks and nomad's sandals. I take care of my feet because the road is long. I feel time as a deep and fast-running river. I follow it. It is the direction that points to the place of our next encounter.

Friend, I hope this letter finds you in good health. Here, as you know, all I lack is the sight of your face. Between my wait and your return lies an expanse of blue sea. I kiss your hands.

I sent this letter telling myself that he would surely find a discreet and faithful reader. My body was cold. I ate a piece of bread and some olives and curled up in a corner, so weary that it was as if I had finally lost all sense of myself. I slept soundly, and the night passed with no encounters with the characters of the stories I was reading.

ASHES
AND
BLOOD

J ust when I thought that I was so free of my past that I no longer even remembered people's faces, my five remaining sisters—one of the seven was seriously ill, perhaps even dead, and another lived abroad—paraded by in a procession even more grotesque than it was ridiculous. Whether this was a vision, a nightmare, a hallucination, or a reality I cannot say. I remember the details clearly, but I cannot seem to locate the time or place.

They were all dressed the same: white shirts, black ties and jellabas, hoods over their heads. They had moustaches drawn in black pencil, and they wore sunglasses. They introduced themselves, one at a time. They each carried plastic bags. Everything seemed identical and carefully rehearsed. The tallest came first, staring at me with bulging eyes. She put the bag on the table and ordered me to open it: inside was a dead rat. I screamed, but my voice made no sound. She held a straight razor in the other hand, ready to slash a face or a throat. I stood pressed against the cold wall, submissive, unable to escape their torture.

The next one, a butcher's knife in her right hand, put the bag down in front of me and gestured to me to open it. Inside was a small box containing a reddish scorpion, live and ready to sting.

The third waved a pair of scissors and held out the bag. It was empty. The moment I opened it she pressed my head against the wall and started to cut my hair. She held her knee against my belly. It hurt. The others laughed and said: "That'll teach you, liar, thief. You took everything from us, you bitch, you murderous bitch."

The fourth—very small, perhaps a dwarf—jumped on me and bit my neck. Blood flowed. I tried to fight back, but the others held me. The dwarf collected the blood in a jar and put it in the plastic bag. "That and the hair will do the trick," she said.

The last one—apparently the youngest—put down her sack between my legs, came toward me with a desolate look, leaned into my arms, and whispered in my ear: "I love you. I don't want them to hurt you. And look, I'm empty-handed. I'm not bad." Then she hit me in the forehead and left with a laugh. So hard was the blow that I almost fainted, but then I felt something brush my legs. This last sister turned out to be the worst. There was a viper in the bag she had left so casually at my feet. I jumped onto the table and howled. By the time I realized where I was, they were all gone. On the ground were a few tufts of hair, drops of blood, and small piles of ash.

I was in tears, deeply shaken. Evil had swooped down on me like the wings of a bird of prey. That story happened to me, though I don't know where or when. Was it in prison, or while my father lay dying? I lived it and relived it in a kind of relentless plague of murky images risen from the darkness. They all had to do with mourning, with a widow despoiled, and with vengeance.

Perhaps it was a nightmare that preceded or followed the punitive expedition of which I was the victim.

One day, as I was deep in darkness in search of the Consul's silhouette, a strong and ugly guard came and took me from my cell. She tore the blindfold from my eyes and made me follow her.

"You have a visitor, and it's not the one you think."

Instead of taking me to the visiting room, she brought me to a cellar, probably a place used for interrogation and torture. She took me to a gray, damp room with a table, a stool, and a lamp.

She left me alone for a few minutes in that room without the tiniest opening for air. Several coats of dark gray paint hid traces of blood on the wall. The door opened and five women filed in, as if in a play, all dressed identically: gray jellabas, white scarves concealing hair and foreheads, gloves, pale faces devoid of all makeup. They were all ugly, and exuded unease. I realized who they were: a sect of Muslim sisters, brutal and fanatical. They gathered around me. I opened my eyes wide and recognized my own sisters. The guard was standing there. They had paid for her complicity and silence. They had come to execute a definite plan, to hurt me, perhaps disfigure me, or simply to threaten and frighten me. The oldest soon explained the intentions of this demented group.

"We have come, five fingers of one hand, to put an end to a situation of usurpation and theft. You were never our brother and you will never be our sister. We have expelled you from the family in the presence of men of religion and witnesses of good faith and high virtue. Now listen to me: you made us believe that you were a statue, a monument radiating light, bringing honor and pride to the house, whereas in fact you were only a hole wrapped in a scrawny body, a hole just like mine and your six ex-sisters'. But you plugged up your hole with wax; you tricked and humiliated us. Just like Father, you held us in contempt. Haughty and arrogant, you ignored us. We would have taken care of you if we could, you last little sister. We would have simply slaughtered you. But God provides. Whoever departs from His path is brought to kneel on a sheet of iron reddened by fire. Now order must be restored. You will not escape. You will pay. There will be no mercy, no respite. Our father lost his reason; our mother, poor woman, fell into the wells of silence; and you took advantage of the calamity, packed your bags and took everything. You left us penniless, in dire poverty, in that ruined old house all moldy, with no more room for life. You ransacked the house and carried off the inheritance. You are in prison now because you deserve it. You ruined the whole family. Now you have to pay. Remember, you are nothing but a hole between two scrawny legs. We are going to plug up that hole forever. You're going to have a circumcision. Not fake this time, but real. Not a cut finger. No, we're going to cut off that little thing that sticks out, and muzzle that hole with a needle and thread. We're going to get rid of that sex you hid. Life will be simpler. No more desire. No more plea-sure. You'll become a thing, a vegetable that will drool until you die. You can start praying. You can shout. No one will hear. Since your betrayal we have discovered the virtues of our beloved religion. Justice has become our passion, truth our ideal and obsession, Islam our guide. We render to life that which belongs to it. And we prefer to act in love and family discretion. Now, in the name of God, the Merciful, the Compassionate, Just and All-Powerful, we open our little case."

As she spoke, two of her companions tied my hands to the icy table. They tore off my saraoul and lifted my legs. The guard, who knew the place well, showed them two hooks in the ceiling and brought them some rope. My legs were held apart, tied on each side. The oldest stuffed a damp rag into my mouth. She put a hand on my belly and crushed the lips of my vagina with her fingers until what they called "the little thing" came out. They sprinkled it with something, took a razor blade from the metal box, soaked it in alcohol, and cut off my clitoris. I fainted, screaming inside.

Excruciating pain woke me in the middle of the night. I was in my cell, my saroual soaked with blood. My sex was sewn up. I knocked on the door to call for help. No one came. I waited until morning and begged one of the guards to take me to the infirmary. I gave her money. The nurse, probably in collusion with the guard-torturer, gave me some ointment and had me sign a paper ac-knowledging that I had mutilated myself. The signature

was the price for the ointment. I realized then that everyone had been corrupted by my sisters. The medicine eased
the pain.

I was lost and bewildered for more than a month, mad,
delirious at night, feverish, on the brink of the abyss. The
Consul had come to see me twice, but I could not bring
myself to speak to him. I hadn't the strength to tell him
what had happened. Yet I was haunted by the idea of
revenge. I thought of several plans, but shame for myself
and disgust with that family brought me back to my crippled and ruined state.

After his second visit, I was able to write a few words
and send them to him through a prisoner who had shown
me some sympathy. This is what I wrote:

> *Lost track of you. Am in darkness and no longer see you.*
> *Sick. Sick. My body wounded. You are my only light.*
> *Thank you.*

THE
FORGOTTEN

W ounded and stricken, I continued my nocturnal wanderings to escape pain more than to seek new encounters. I cleared myself a path between skeletal bodies hanging in a huge warehouse. They dangled naked and transparent, the skin stretched over their bones. It was an army of bodies emptied of all substance. I saw a door at the other end of the warehouse. I went to it. There was an exit sign in several languages, with green arrows. I followed the arrows. But I never reached the exit. I wandered in that vast barracks of bodies, amid icy silence and the smell of fear. I never knew that fear could have a smell. There was a slight draught, which made the bodies sway ever so slightly. Sometimes bones clacked together, the sound amplified by the echo. I heard a voice behind me:

"Come closer, I have just enough time to reveal the secret of life and to tell you of the face of death. Don't be afraid. They thought I was dead. I was only wounded, but I can already see the landscape of the afterlife. Are you wounded too? I have nothing to fear anymore. I want you to know, I want everyone to know. Wait, don't go!"

I turned and saw a man with blood on his knees; his face had a greenish cast. He was not a jinni, but a dying man. He was straining to tell me some secret. I moved closer:

"All the people you see here were poor; beggars and tramps, diseased. One day an order was given to clean up the town for an important visitor, a foreigner who was to take a short walk in the streets. We were the dirty, unacceptable face of the country, whose image had to be polished. So we had to be sent away, at least temporarily, during the few days of the foreigner's visit. The order was carried out. There were raids. They stuck us all here and completely forgot us. We fought among ourselves. I am the last survivor, the one who has to disappear because his testimony is so horrible. Tell everybody what you have seen here. This is no nightmare. We are not ghosts. We are human castoffs, forever forgotten. No one came to claim us. You are the first human being to enter this warehouse."

I had no doubt stumbled into that place, drawn there by my sharp pain. I was awake, and this was a vision. It was all true. It had happened in winter. The townspeople still talk about it. All those bodies were discovered on the day the fairgrounds were opened for a new show. There was more fear than pain. Fear and disgust. I felt my body. The flesh and bones were bruised. I tried not to urinate, because I knew it would hurt. My belly was swollen. When I finally urinated I held my breath. I was sweating. The dying man's voice entered me and merged with mine until it became my own voice. I could no longer hear the dying man, but I spoke inside myself, endlessly repeating what he had told me. Strangely, this eased the intensity of my pain.

I spent two nights mired in fever, pain, and fear.

My mutilation was a form of vengeance. But how had my sisters come by such a barbarous idea? I later discovered that the torture inflicted on me is a commonly practiced operation in Black Africa and in parts of Egypt and the Sudan. Its effect is to deprive young girls just awakening to life of any possibility of desire and pleasure. I also learned that neither Islam nor any other religion has ever permitted this kind of slaughter.

The dying man's voice that dwelled within me became clear and precise:

"The guard is a slave brought long ago from the Sudan. She is a witch, an expert in torture."

It must have been she who suggested to my sisters that they make me an invalid and expel me definitively from life.

The persistent fever was due to infection. Rage flowed in my blood. My visions became more and more sinister. My voice changed. I felt possessed by death. To rid myself of it I had to report what I had seen in the warehouse. I looked for someone to talk to. Not a guard or a nurse. I was lucky, for as I was dragging myself up to go to the sick bay, I collapsed in the corridor just as a doctor was passing. I was half-conscious. He was furious. He shouted that they were all savages and barbarians. Someone from the prison administration showed him the declaration in which I acknowledged that I had mutilated myself. He became even more violently angry. I was taken straight to the hospital, where he treated me for the infection and waited several days before removing, under anesthetic, the stitches that had sewn up the lips of my vagina. When I told him how it had happened, he found it hard to believe. He wanted to call the police, but a moment later he raised his arms in a gesture of impotence.

"Everyone here is corrupt," he said. "No one will believe your story. The police won't challenge what the guards say. Besides which, there is the paper you signed. But why? What did you do to those women?"

He reassured me that my general health was sound and promised to do all he could to keep me in the hospital as long as possible.

"At least it's better than prison," he said.

Despite the medicines, I was still in pain. I was convinced that I would continue to suffer until I revealed what I had seen in the warehouse—seen or imagined. Those images and the words of the dying man weighed heavily on me mentally and physically. Every word was like a sharp glass needle piercing my body's every sensitive point.

I asked the doctor if he could spare me a moment after work. At first he hesitated, but finally agreed. I began by warning him of the extraordinary nature of my visions, explaining that even if they did not really exist, they were still affecting me.

"I am not insane," I said, "but I live in a world without

much logic. Believe me, all I ask is that you hear me out."

I told him in detail of my nocturnal wanderings. He did not seem surprised. He nodded as if there was nothing unusual about my tale. When I finished, he got up and said:

"You may not really have seen all this, but it is true. The police did lock up beggars and then forget about them. The press never mentioned it. But here rumor is a sure source of information. Everybody knew, but no one went to check, so it became an incredible story. What I find astonishing is the connection between your suffering and this incident."

"Great pain affords me a lucidity that borders on clairvoyance. Let's put it that way."

I felt much better after that session. I did not think of the Consul during those days. I had not forgotten him, but I was determined not to involve him in these stories of blood and death. He did not know of my hospitalization. When he came to the prison, he was told that I did not want to see him. He suspected something. He thought I was sick or depressed, that I dared not let him see my gloomy, joyless face. He clung tightly to that version of things. When he came to the hospital, this was the first thing he said to me:

"Are you ready to show me your face now?"

He was far from suspecting the bloody ordeal I had just suffered.

His first act was to look at my face. He sat on the edge of the bed and gently caressed my forehead, cheeks, nose, mouth, and chin.

"You have cried a lot and you've lost weight. You mustn't neglect yourself! It's not good."

157

The doctor took him aside and told him why I was in the hospital. He didn't say anything to me about it. He held my hand and squeezed it hard. When he left, I ran my fingers over my cheeks; they felt gritty. My face looked terrible. I had not washed in several days. That evening I locked myself in the bathroom and did something about my appearance.

The Consul came to see me often. He brought flowers, fruit, perfume. He never came empty-handed. He never mentioned what had happened. I appreciated his discretion, yet it also disturbed me. How was I to interpret his silence? Was it an expression of sympathy, of solidarity, or was it a sign of embarrassment slowly digging a furrow between us? It was hard for me to broach the subject. When he came, he would ask me whether I was sleeping well and then move on to something else. Sometimes he talked to the doctor, but not in my presence. I later found out that one of the things he was obsessed with was whether I could still have children. That tormented him, though he did not show it. I thought about it too. Earlier I had rejected any idea of pregnancy, birth, and bringing up children. I never had time to consider the notion of being a mother. I admit that the thought had never even crossed my mind on the few occasions I had had sexual relations with the Consul. Which gives some idea of how new to me it all was and how much I still considered my body a sandbag. I saw myself as a straw scarecrow who attracted crows instead of scaring them away, some happily nesting on my shoulders, others even pecking holes where the eyes were. I was losing any sense of my presence in the world. I felt as if I was crumbling into ruins, and endlessly putting myself together again. Everything was confused. I was looking for some way to ease the pain, not only the pain that coursed through my veins like poison, but also the pain I was beginning to feel after the Consul's visits. He would come and sit in silence. His presence weighed tons. He seemed overwhelmed, unhappiness dwelling within him. I was increasingly disoriented, disturbed, sinking into confusion and nightmarish visions. I was alone again, without anesthetic, facing the final reverses of fortune, disaster, sadness, and violence showing me no mercy. I decided to go back to the prison. Partial freedom in the midst of all that whiteness was too cruel for my eyes to bear. I had to beg the doctor to send me back to my cell.

I was getting ready to leave when the Consul came in. He looked a little less sad than usual. He had a sprig of mint with him.

"Let's make some tea, as we used to," he said.

I had a powerful feeling, leaving no room for doubt, that something had finally broken between us. I couldn't say why, but I felt it, and was not surprised.

We didn't make the tea. I told him I was going back to prison. He said nothing. He sat in a chair. I was on the edge of the bed. I noticed he was blushing.

"Please stop moving," he said.

"I'm not moving."

"I know, but there's such a lot of traffic in your head. I can hear your thoughts rattling around." Then he said, in a tone more calm:

"My hands don't have the strength to look at you today. They're tired. They feel useless and guilty. I feel remorse that I have never measured up to your enthusiasm and courage. I am condemned never to feel enthusiasm. Ever since childhood I have been mired in tragedy, and my orders from heaven or from life itself forced me to persevere, not to cut the thread of life, to consolidate my being, making it normal. I can't seem to tell you everything I think and believe with any real coherence. I accepted the Seated Woman's death, but not your departure and imprisonment. Ever since then I have been relentlessly seeking some shelter, some place of peace for my thoughts and for my weary body. I try to open the sealed lips of my mother underground. To hear her voice just once, to hear her bless me or even curse me, but just to hear her. I know I have to travel in darkness, in the distant desert, in the Far South. I am writing now, and you are dictating to me. What I write scares me, possesses me. Where do you get that power to go through life, disrupting it with such arrogance, such courage? When I used to write for myself, I did it at night. But now your fraught voice comes to me in the morning. Your thoughts cross the night and arrive in the early hours. It is my task to organize and transcribe them. I add very little. Your story is terrifying. You yourself are the secret that possesses me. I can free myself of it only by pressing on to the story's very end. But what will I find then? You are not the type to end a story. You're more the type to leave it open, in order to make it an endless tale. Your story is a series of doors opening onto white spaces and spinning labyrinths. Sometimes you come upon a meadow, sometimes a ruined old house closed in on its occupants, all long dead. The place of your birth perhaps, a cursed place struck by the law of absence and oblivion. My friend! Since I have become your voice, borne by it to silk-wrapped, bloodstained nights, my world has been strange. I am sure I'm not imagining all this. I am verging on your gift of clairvoyance. How can I tell you that to reach you I must pass through a narrow door? I hear you, my hands seek you out. But I know you are far away, on another continent, closer to the full moon than to my gaze. Yet I see you, now a man, now a woman, superb creature of childhood, eluding love and friendship. You are out of reach, a being of darkness, shadow in the night of my sufferings. Sometimes I cry out unconsciously, 'Who are you?' Sometimes I feel that since the tragedy I have been trapped in a spell cast by your family, woven by wicked hands. I would like to ask you, even to beg you, to remain what you are, to press on, for neither prison nor others' tears will stop you. I waited so long for you. You came into my life with the strange grace of a lost animal. With you my heart became a home. Since you left, I have ceased to live there. My loneliness is stark, no longer protected by your care. Your voice alone animates my body, and I write. However terrified, I transcribe what you tell me. I have come to say goodbye and to ask forgiveness. Our story has become impossible. I will continue to live it elsewhere, in some other way. I am going away, going where my blindness will become a mere infirmity again, a gloomy fate I could not escape despite your visit. But I want you to know that I have learned your beauty with my hands, and that this has moved me like a child who first looks upon the sea. I will take care of my hands, I will cover them with fine cloth, for they bear the imprint of your beauty like a secret. I am telling you this because I have also learned that the peculiar quality of this emotion is that it is unique. I close my eyes and hands around it and keep it forever. Farewell, my friend!"

MY
STORY,
MY PRISON

T|he Consul's confession left me perplexed, though I was sure of one thing: my story, which had made me a child of sand and wind, would pursue me all my life, leaving no room for anything else. Everything that would ever happen to me would be an extension of it, a direct or disguised manifestation of it in one form or another.

My story was my prison; that I was locked in a gray cell for killing a man was secondary. I carried my prison like a shell on my back wherever I went. Perhaps the isolation might help me sever the threads woven around me by that twisted destiny. I was a closed box kept in some tight, sealed shed. A stifling torpor pressed down

163

on me from so far off that I felt I had suffered the ordeal for centuries.

The Consul had left me a sheet of paper folded in four. I opened it. On it was a drawing, or rather a road map. An arrow pointed clumsily to the south, another to the north. In the middle was a palm tree, and not far away some waves drawn like birds with outstretched wings. On the back of the sheet of paper he had written this:

> Friendship alone, total gift of the soul, absolute light, light on light, the body barely visible. Friendship is grace; it is my religion, our territory; friendship alone will give your body back its mistreated soul. Follow your heart, follow the emotion that runs in your blood. Farewell, my friend!

After that I abandoned my blindfold and my wanderings in the darkness. I began to be obsessed with the idea of a great light from the sky, a light so strong it would make my body transparent, cleanse it, restore to it the pleasure of astonishment, the innocence of knowing the beginning of things. The idea excited me. I devoted myself entirely to developing it, until the Consul's image was lost, becoming hazy and elusive. I had lost track of him.

I found life in prison natural. I forgot the need for freedom. Being shut in did not oppress me. I now felt receptive. Women came to see me, brought me letters to write for them. I was happy to do favors, to be useful. I was given a small desk, paper and pens. I had become confidant and counselor. My only recompense was an inner satisfaction, something to do that took me away from my own prison. Meanwhile, my nights increasingly resembled a house people were moving out of. Little by little they were emptied of their dubious, often monstrous tenants, as all the characters I had accumulated during my life were asked to leave. I evicted them without hesitation. The moment I closed my eyes I saw them leaving like so many ghosts getting off a train in a thick fog. Some protested, others threatened to come back for revenge. They were taken by surprise by my sudden lack of hospitality. I noticed that they all seemed crippled, half-awake, nonplussed. They dragged their feet. There was even a legless man moving very fast and punching the laggards as he passed. They should have been happy to leave that rotting carcass. My nights were becoming more and more like an unused railway platform. The characters were lost in the darkness as they fell from my nights. I heard their footsteps fading, then there was silence, with the occasional sound of someone falling.

My days were filled with my work as public scribe. I spent the night cleaning up, for they left behind piles of old things that stuck in my memory and gave me no peace.

It had taken a long time—months—to clean out the inside of my head. Among the images I lost was the Consul's. Yet I never saw him leave. I only knew that he was no longer inside me. Only the memory of our entwined bodies cropped up vividly from time to time. You can forget a face, but can never really wipe out the memory of the warmth of an emotion, the sweetness of a gesture, the sound of a tender voice.

My phase of activity won me official recognition by the prison administration as "public scribe and secretary." I also had to draft letters for the warden. As a prison functionary, albeit an inmate, I had to wear regulation dress:

gray jacket and trousers, blue shirt, black tie, navy blue cap, black shoes.

At first these accoutrements bothered me. But I had no choice. It was a request, but it sounded like an order. The work, especially in uniform, helped me to take some distance from myself. The Consul's image continued to fade until it became a shifting point in the center of a flame. My memories were falling away; I was losing them gradually the way others lose their hair. My head gleamed, no memory sticking to it.

When I put on my uniform in the morning, I would look at myself in the mirror and smile. I was wearing men's clothes again. But it was no longer a disguise. These were work clothes. The women dressed like the men so as to look harsh and to bolster their authority. I didn't give anyone orders, yet the prisoners greeted me as though I were their superior. It was ridiculous. Some called me "sir," perhaps not on purpose. I did not correct them. I let that doubt stand, but my conscience was clear. I wasn't fooling anyone. I took care of my face. I used more makeup than before. I had become coquettish. People in prison continue to play on appearances despite everything, but I no longer had the heart to play.

Little by little my conditions improved. I was granted some privileges. I was considered neither fully a prisoner, nor a prison employee like the others. I was envied by some, feared by others. I came and went between the two camps as though I was written in two languages.

When there were few letters to write, I gathered together those prisoners who were still interested in life outside and I read to them from several-day-old newspapers. Earth-shaking events—wars, coups d'état—did

166

not affect them. They wanted the crime and human-interest stories. "Blood! Love!" they would shout. Crimes of passion were their favorites. The reading sessions turned into storytelling evenings. I would make them up as I went along. The basic plot was always the same: an impossible love ending in bloodshed. I took pleasure in creating characters and situations. Sometimes I wandered so far afield that the audience protested, making fun of my commentaries. What they wanted were the bare facts. When the audience got too noisy, I would stop the story. But my storytelling talent soon ran dry. I began to tell the same tale again and again. It was about two secret lovers facing risk and danger. Then came tragedy: discovery, punishment, and vengeance.

Some women came to me privately and told me the story of their lives. They made a lot of it up. They thought their lives were novels, that they suffered the fate of misunderstood heroines. In prison words were all they had left, and they used them and misused them. They invented stories full of adventure. I listened patiently. I had not had much experience of life. I learned a lot through those stories about the mores of my society, about the meanness of men, and about the greatness and weakness of the soul. I realized how sheltered I had been during childhood and youth, how far I had been from the wind, cold, and hunger. It was as if my father had kept me under a glass, protected from dust and people's touch. It was hard to breathe, because I wore a mask of steel and was trapped in a family that was itself trapped in sickness, fear, and madness. Had I been a girl among girls, my fate might have been violent, but not wretched, not tainted with shame, theft, and lies.

167

Between the gray walls I could not stop pondering these tales of woe. My gaze lost its balance and wandered at random. Sometimes I felt useless, and that made me deeply angry. I was back in the cursed place where my father was buried. I turned into an evil shadow. I dug him up and stepped on him. I was insane. When I thought about being released, I felt sick, broke out in sweats.

With time and the habits of everyday life, things died away inside me: my fits of rage disappeared, my feelings were blank with the whiteness that leads to nothingness and slow death. My emotions had been dissolved in a lake of stagnant water. My body had stopped developing; it no longer changed. It was fading, no longer able to move or feel. It was neither a woman's body full and eager, nor a man's serene and strong. I was now somewhere between the two; in other words, in hell.

HELL

They had been walking for a long time. Since sunrise. In silence. You could see them in the distance, women coming forward in small groups. They came from afar, some from the north, others from the east. Their desire to reach that dune, to enter that mythical place, source of all light, concealed the hunger, thirst, and exhaustion on their faces. Their lips were cracked by the heat and wind; some were bleeding from the nose; they all accepted these annoyances, with no weariness, no regrets. They walked in the sand until they merged with its movements, bearing their shadows like a standard to hail the final dune, to forget the dry wind and the morning chill, to arrive just at the moment when the light turns soft and ambiguous, when it drifts away from the sun and joins the sky on the threshold of night. They had to arrive at exactly that instant of indeterminate duration. I, in my solitude, had decided that eternity would begin here. Any walk would have to end and melt into that light. The desert had its laws, and grace its secrets.

The women making that journey asked no questions. They knew they had to arrive just at the moment when light makes the passage from day to night. That was one of the conditions for acceptance of their request to the Holy Woman.

I was holy and merciless. Now a statue, now a mummy, I ruled. My memory was gone, and I came from nowhere. My blood must be white. My eyes changed color with the sun.

Most of them were young. Accompanied by their mothers or aunts, they dared not look into the sun. They had to look down, staring at the sand silently marked by their feet in their thick, woolen socks.

They had heard talk of the Holy Woman of the sands, daughter of light, whose hands had grace and the power to halt the irremediable, to ward off misfortune, and perhaps even to prevent sterility in young women. They came here after all else had failed. I was their last resort.

It all had to happen in silence. The silence in that place had the color of dry ice, something like blue. It spread like a light slithering between stones. Only a distant echo, a child's cry, dwelled permanently in their minds.

I sat on a throne, wearing white gloves, my face veiled. One by one the women crossed the room on their knees, heads lowered, until they were half a yard from me. They

170

kissed my hand and raised their dresses. I had to stroke their flat bellies softly and brush their pubes.

I took off the glove and passed on the warmth that was supposed to assure them fertility. Sometimes my fingers ploughed their bellies as if they were soft, damp soil. The women were happy; some gripped my hand and slid it toward their vaginas. They thought that caresses were not enough. To make doubly sure they forced my fingers to bruise their skin, even to wound it. I was tireless. The women filed in all night. The Law of this place and of an omnipotent but invisible master was that they had to leave at dawn, at first light. I was perplexed by the very young women who were brought to me. They were sometimes so young that I dared not touch them. I simply dipped my fingers in a bowl of argan oil and barely touched their lips. Some licked my fingers, others turned away, perhaps finding the oil's strong smell unpleasant. Often their mothers would slap them on the back of the neck, forcing them to rub their faces in my hand.

Later I came to know hell. It was one of those clear nights when everything is larger than life: sounds were louder, objects moved, faces changed, and I felt lost and brutalized.

I was seated as usual, my hand ready for the ritual. I went through the motions mechanically. Everything seemed unsettled, false, immoral, and grotesque. Suddenly silence fell over the dune. The women were lined up to receive the key of their deliverance from my hand.

Hell was inside me, with its disorder, its hallucinations, and its madness.

The naked belly before me was hairy. I lowered my

hand slightly and found an erect penis. I took my hand away and looked at the face that was trying to hide from me. In a low voice he said:

"You went away long ago. Why did you leave us so suddenly? You left us only your shadow. I could not sleep anymore. I looked for you everywhere. Give yourself back! Give me back my breath, my life, the strength to be a man. Your power is immense. The whole country knows it. You went away long ago. Put your hand on my belly again. You can even tear it with your nails. If I have to suffer, let it be at your hands. You are beautiful and inaccessible. Why have you turned away from life, why do you sit in death's shadow?"

The hood of his jellaba was pulled down over his head. I was afraid of what I might find. Perhaps that voice was known to me. I did not have to raise the hood. He did it himself. The face changed color and shape. Images were piled one atop the other, forming now a picture of my father, now that of the uncle I had killed. Suddenly the image of the Consul appeared to me in those ancient faces, his eyes open, shining and laughing, eyes bright, perhaps even blue. The man was no longer talking to me. He stared at me. I had to lower my eyes. I leaned forward and kissed his hands. I had no wish to speak. I felt all the warmth of his body rising within me, a warmth that came from his open gaze, from his eyes freed of darkness. That gust of heat tore my eyebrows away tuft by tuft, then my eyelashes, then pieces of the skin of my forehead.

I felt a pain in my belly, then an emptiness, rising persistently within me. I was bare-headed, my shoulders scorched, my hands immobilized. And I suffered time and its misfortunes, unknown to the rest of the world, as if that man and I were locked in a glass cage. I was a failure and I walked alone on a road paved with marble where I might fall at any moment. I realized that I was coming out of myself, that the entire scene would have to lead to this departure in a ravaged body. I was filled with old rags, delivered to that light that was supposed to be beautiful. But I had no strength and no feeling; I was burned from inside, hurled into the whirlpool of emptiness. It was white all around me. "So this is death," I said to myself, somewhat hesitant. "A barefoot journey on cold marble, wrapped in a sheet of mist or white clouds. It is not unpleasant. But where is the end? Will I spend eternity in this burning light that leaves me no shade? This is not death, then, but hell!"

A voice, unknown but clear, spoke to me: "One day you will give birth to a bird of prey, who will perch on your shoulder and show you the path. One day the sun will sink a little closer to you. You will not escape it. It will leave your body intact, but will burn everything in it. One day the mountain will open and will carry you off. If you are a man, it will keep you; if you are a woman, it will grant you a robe of stars and will send you to the land of endless love . . . One day . . . One day . . ."

The voice was gone. Perhaps it was my own voice, taken from me by another. They must have taken my voice and left it to wander in the clouds. Then it spoke to itself all alone. I was unable to say a single word. My voice was gone, but I heard it in the distance, coming from somewhere else, crossing other mountains. My voice was free. But I was still a prisoner.

———

My sleepless nights were peopled by images of those women in white walking laboriously in the sand. They headed toward a white point on the horizon. Would they someday reach that place that exists only in my madness? And even if, by some miracle, the hand of fortune led them to a holy woman's tomb, they would then stand facing a hoax. I know this now, but cannot tell them. They would not believe me anyway. I am only a criminal who must serve her sentence, using this imagery to outwit ennui. But suffering—the kind that bores holes in head and heart—cannot be spoken or displayed. It lies within, locked away and invisible.

I had no need of these new visions born of burns and fever to batter down fate's heavy door. I would get out, I sensed that, but I did not want to leave prison burdened with all those tormenting images. How could I get rid of them? How could I consign them to the gray stones of my cell?

I put the black blindfold on my eyes again, undressed, and lay flat on the ground. I was completely naked. The cement was icy. My body warmed it.

I was shivering. I had sworn that I would resist the cold. I had to endure that ordeal to cast off the images. I had to remind my body of the site of my confinement, to recall that there could be no escape through dreams become nightmares.

If the soul were flayed, the body could tell no more lies. I fell asleep despite the damp and cold that gnawed at my skin. My night was long and beautiful. And free of all images. In the morning I was coughing, but I felt better.

THE
SAINT

I wept as I left prison, my sentence commuted. I was glad that my eyes were wet with tears, for it had been so long since that had happened. They were happy tears, because they came from a body being reborn, a body once again capable of feelings, of emotion. I wept because I was leaving a world where I had succeeded in finding a place. I wept because no one was waiting for me. I was free. And alone. I thought of the Consul, but I knew he had left town, that he had gone far away, to a place where he might free himself of our story.

I yearned to see the sea, to smell its scent, see its color, touch its foam. I took a bus headed south. We drove all night. People smoked and drank lemonade. My eyes stayed open, waiting for the sea. Early in the morning I saw a light mist rising from the earth like a vast sheet stretched over the ground, a sheet or an expanse of snow. Then I glimpsed ships and sailboats. They seemed almost suspended, hanging over a patch of fog. The bottom of the air was white and soft. Everything had a kind of innocence, a magic that made them seem near and inoffensive. Objects were vague, undefined. Perhaps my sight had not adjusted yet. Dreams must take their images from that whitish layer crossed by rays of blue.

It was autumn. I was wearing a man's jellaba of thick, rough wool. My hair was covered by a pretty, brightly colored scarf. I put on lipstick, and black kohl around my eyes. I looked at myself in a little mirror. My face was slowly coming back to life, lighting up from inside. I was happy and carefree. I looked funny in my truckdriver's jellaba. The drowsing passengers looked uneasily at me. I smiled at them, and they looked away. Men cannot stand being looked at by a woman in this country. They like to stare, of course, but always obliquely.

The bus station was opposite the sea. Step over a low wall and you were on sand. I walked slowly along the deserted beach, moving through the mist. I could see only a few yards ahead. I looked back and felt hemmed in by the belt of mist; a white veil separated me from the rest of the world. I was alone, cloistered in the happy solitude that comes before a great event. I took off my slippers. The sand was damp. A slight, fresh wind from afar pushed me along. I let myself be carried like a leaf. Suddenly a powerful, almost unbearable light came down from the sky, so violent that I thought I glimpsed a floating balloon, the source of that light. It drove the fog away. I felt naked. Now there was nothing to protect me. Opposite me, on the now miraculously close horizon, I saw a white house perched on a rock. I scaled the stones and reached the top. The sea was before me, the sand behind me. The house was open. There was no door. It had only one, very large room. No furniture. Old, worn mats covered the floor. Hanging oil lamps would have provided faint light at night. In one corner were some men. Some were asleep, others prayed silently. There were women and children on the other side. Only one old lady was praying. I went across and stared at her. Absorbed in her prayers, she did not see me. I sat down beside her and pretended to pray. But I made a wrong gesture, and that drew her attention. She was strangely like the Seated Woman. Less fat, but with the same movements, the same way of sitting. I stopped praying and looked at her anxiously. She was telling her beads, her lips barely moving. Our eyes met, and a moment later she leaned toward me and said, her beads still clicking:

"Here you are at last!"

It was she! The Seated Woman! Her voice had not changed. Her face had a few more wrinkles, but it was calmer now, more human.

I recoiled for an instant, then said without thinking:

"Yes, here I am!"

I was in the grip of some spell. I was about to say something when she took me by the arm.

"Speak softly," she said, "or you'll wake the Saint."

Now everything was becoming clear. Between life and death, I thought, there was but a thin layer of mist or darkness; the threads of lies were woven between reality and appearance, while time was but an illusion born of our own anguish.

The Saint rose later than everyone else. He came out of a door at the back. Dressed all in white, he wore a veil and dark glasses. Men and women alike rushed to kiss his hand. Sometimes a man lingered near him, apparently to whisper some secret. The Saint would nod, then reassure him as if to bless him.

I too got up and joined the line of women. But then, in a playful mood, I crossed to the line of men. In my jellaba I could pass for a man. When I reached the Saint, I knelt, took his outstretched hand, and instead of kissing it, licked it, sucking each of his fingers. The Saint tried to pull his hand away, but I held it in both of mine. He seemed troubled. I rose and whispered in his ear:

"It has been so long since a man caressed my face. Go ahead, look softly at me with your fingers, with the palm of your hand."

He leaned toward me and said:

"You're here at last!"